For Donna

With appreciation
for all of your help.
You do a great job!

Phyllis Hurst

The Last Leaf
Has Fallen

The Last Leaf Has Fallen

J. Willis Hurst, MD

Library of Congress Control Number:		2007907099
ISBN:	Hardcover	978-1-4257-9848-2
	Softcover	978-1-4257-9828-4

This book was printed in the United States of America.

To order additional copies of this book, contact:
Xlibris Corporation
1-888-795-4274
www.Xlibris.com
Orders@Xlibris.com
42254

For Nelie with love

PREFACE

Hippocrates, the father of modern medicine, lived, practiced, and taught on the Greek island of Kos about 460 years before the birth of Christ. A descendant of the tree under which he taught still stands. In our mind's eye, let us imagine that the tree symbolizes the profession of medicine. Let us examine it. The *roots*, which symbolize the ethical and scientific basis of medicine, are beginning to show a moderate amount of damage. The *leaves*, which represent physicians, are disappearing! Thinking people wonder why the roots of the tree have deteriorated and why the leaves are vanishing.

The pages of this book of fiction relate several intertwining themes. Although he has not retired, Dr. Vance Connelly, whose wife has recently died, moves to an excellent nationally accredited retirement community known as Brookland Square. He leaves his new apartment each day at 5:00 AM in order to teach medical students, house officers, and fellows at the internationally recognized Greystone University Hospital. He writes for the remainder of his eight-hour workday and returns to his apartment by 3:00 PM. Vance

Connelly formerly chaired the Department of Medicine but continues to work despite his age of eighty-five. He keeps up with many of his former house officers and, in this book, tracks two of them who have had very different careers. Eventually one of them seems to be the only doctor left who fits the definition of a truly professional doctor. The other one wanders far from his training and succumbs to greed.

There are many good doctors, but they are currently forced to work in a bad system. They have lost control of their actions and destiny. *This, in turn, is breaking the compassionate spirit of the strongest among them.* In addition, the same external forces are driving some doctors out of the profession they love and are interfering with the humanitarian action of many others. This too is discussed in this book.

The book describes behind-the-scenes views of certain aspects of the famous teaching hospital, the Greystone University Hospital; an unbiased look at the life of elderly people who live at Brookland Square; the ruthlessness of a pharmaceutical house; the lives of two very different doctors, Dan Baldwin and Gerald Colfax, who trained with Dr. Vance Connelly; and, most importantly, the love affair between Vance Connelly and his wife Jennifer.

St. Simons Island (January 16, 2005)

ACKNOWLEDGMENTS

A portion of this book is true, and another part is sheer make-believe. The parts of the book that relate to Greystone University Hospital, the Brookland Square retirement community, Middleton, and Vance Connelly's love affair with Jennifer are true. Most names have been changed. The events did not happen in the sequence that is presented, but they happened. The story of the two doctors and the pharmaceutical house MediSurge is pure fiction. It did not happen, but it could.

The short passage from a graduation address that is quoted in chapter 1 was previously published in 1995 by Raven Press in my book *Essays from the Heart*, for which I hold the copyright.

I thank Libby Christian for typing draft after draft after draft of the manuscript. She is able to change my scribbles into sentences with apparent ease. I'm deeply indebted to Lynda Prickett Mathews for her assistance in adding the final touches to the book. I am also deeply indebted to Ruth Griffin, who is an excellent grammarian, for reading and correcting every sentence of the manuscript. Her eagle eye discovered many errors and poor syntax. This, in turn, led to their correction, which improved the manuscript considerably. Finally, I express my appreciation to the staff at Xlibris who proved their competence at every step of the way.

CHAPTER 1

May 1, 2004
Blackland Road, Atlanta, Georgia

Dr. Vance Connelly struggled to get his breath. The breathlessness came in spells as waves of gloom overpowered him. He sat alone in the living room of his home, which was located on Blackland Road in Buckhead, one of the most affluent suburbs of Atlanta.

Boxes were all around the grey-haired and properly wrinkled eighty-three-year-old physician. He sat in an armchair with one hand supporting his head, pondering which box to open. His eyes were red from crying. He removed his glasses for a moment, pinched the bridge of his nose, and closed his eyes. But this was not followed by peace or comfort—only more grief. The ordeal was beyond his tolerance. His three sons and their wives had helped him pack many cherished things from many rooms of his home into the boxes so that he could sit quietly—alone—and examine their contents at his leisure. Some of the boxes contained memorabilia of his work at Greystone University Hospital; and others, such as photographs and letters, reminded him of his long life with Jennifer.

Vance felt tears on his cheeks. He wiped them away, but they returned. He could not, he believed, go on without her. Jennifer, his devoted wife—his life—had died on April 26, 2004, from a pulmonary complication of surgery that was performed for a deadly cancer of the pancreas.

Vance thought, *I must describe the emotion of grief. After all, as a teaching doctor, I am supposed to be able to detect and describe the emotions of patients. Surely, I should be able to describe what I, myself, am feeling.*

But descriptive words failed him. He could not tell others how he felt. The waves of an oppressive feeling overwhelmed him. Some of the waves almost suffocated him. Jennifer had been the strong one all during their long marriage. She was mainly responsible for rearing their three successful sons. She had made their house a home, but she was now in heaven improving the place. Vance realized that she had died but could not believe it. She was so beautiful, so stable, and so caring. The beautiful red hair of her youth gradually changed to auburn with a few streaks of gray, but it was still beautiful. Vance always realized that he could not have been chairman of Greystone's Department of

Medicine without her help. She had faced her final days with courage. Vance slept in the hospital to be near her during her three months of illness. Their talking time was brief because her medical care required the use of an endotracheal tube. She struggled for three months against an enemy known as acute respiratory disease syndrome (ARDS). During the brief period when she was able to talk, she spoke without tears—as each of them said I love you. She also pointed out that Vance could not remain in the home they both loved when she could no longer be there. Such a thought pulled Vance's heartstrings from his body. To be without her and the house they both loved was unthinkable.

Vance sat and looked at the boxes but could not force himself to open them. He sat lost in the memory of the first time he saw Jennifer. She was walking with books in her arms with two other girls. She was seventeen years old. She wore a faintly purple dress. Vance later told his mother that he saw the girl he wanted to marry, and he did five years later. This led to a flashback of their years of happiness together. Then grief overwhelmed him again.

An hour later, Vance began to look in the boxes. Old letters from him to Jennifer brought audible sounds of moaning that broke the silence. Letters from her to him took his breath away.

An old manuscript was in one of the boxes. Vance had written it when he was the honoree of the Atlanta Heart Ball in 1985. Vance relived the night. He recalled that he thanked the appropriate people for the honor they had bestowed upon him and indicated how pleased he was that they had raised a lot of money for heart research. He then turned to Jennifer and said,

It is spring now and the dogwoods of our city will make a fairyland for us to enjoy. And in the spring a young man's fancy turns to love. Whereas I am old enough to halt my hand, I am young enough to want to dangle your name—Jennifer—from the back of an airplane—or place it in large letters on the billboards around town—or to place it on the screen at the stadium, even when the Braves are losing again, to proclaim my love for you. So, Jennifer, in my mind's eye, your name is there. You have made our house a home. You guided me and our three sons with great devotion, love, and skill. You have been my anchor when I was drifting and my rudder when the water was turbulent.

All of you here can be assured that without her, your honoree would be someone else tonight. No Jennifer, no me.

A second manuscript caught Vance's eye. It was a graduation speech he had given at Greystone University School of Medicine in 1990. Jennifer was there when he advised the graduates as follows:

You will have to struggle to know what the truth is. While this has always been difficult, it is more difficult now. The gentle persuasion of sophisticated hype will lead you by the nose unless you guard against it.

It will be increasingly easy and painless for you to step over the ethical lines you can draw today. So I ask you to draw the lines clearly before the sun sets and never yield to the temptations that will be offered to you every day of your life.

My wife, Jennifer, is in the audience. If it were not for her loving care, I would not be here today. So, prejudiced by my own experience, I recommend that you choose

an understanding partner to travel the road
that is ahead of you. Should you be as lucky
as I have been, the demons of this world will
be no match for such a partnership, and the
pleasures that are always around you will be
greatly enhanced.

He saw a small cardboard box of photographs that
had been taken in the same room where he sat. Early
in his career, Vance had an annual house staff party in
his home for the interns and residents. Jennifer was a
gracious hostess. In order for all members of the house
staff to attend, it was necessary to have the party on two
consecutive nights. As the department grew in size, it
would have been necessary to have the party three or
four nights in a row. This, of course, was not practical.
So with regret, Vance and Jennifer moved the party
to another location. Photographs were taken at each
party, and Vance held one of them in his hand. It was
a picture of two residents who worked together. One
was named Dan Baldwin, and the other one was named
Gerald Colfax. When they finished their training, they
joined each other in practice in Savannah, Georgia.
Vance would occasionally stop by to see them when
he and Jennifer traveled to their condominium, which
was located on St. Simons Island. Vance remembered

that he had read something about them recently in the *Atlanta Journal-Constitution*. He concluded that he would check on them later, but now was not the time.

Vance finally looked through three boxes. There were five boxes left, but he could not force himself to look in them—not now, maybe later.

Vance saw his old friend Johnny standing near the window. Vance struggled to lift himself from the chair, reached for his cane, and slowly walked to the door to open it. He said, "Sorry, Johnny, you know I have a hearing problem. I did not hear the doorbell."

He opened the door to greet his college roommate, Johnny Hendrick, who lived at Brookland Square, one of the city's well-known retirement communities.

Johnny looked the same except for the color of his hair. He had always combed it back without a part. His hair was snow white now whereas it was formerly jet-black, and his belt size was a bit larger than it was when they were in college. Johnny held out his hand. "Man, I know what you are going through. You know I have been there. I just wanted to come by and help if I can." With that he wiped a tear from his cheek.

"Thanks, Johnny, but you know . . . you know how terrible it is."

"I do. I do. You know I do. Why don't you move over to Brookland? You can't stay here. I checked all of the places out—Brookland is the best. It has met my needs."

Vance responded, "Jennifer and I had talked about that. She just could not bear to leave our home. But during her terminal illness, she insisted that I must."

Johnny left, saying, "Well, anyway, I will be back. Call me if you need me."

Vance reflected on their college days. They had roomed together in a run-down fraternity house and courted two beautiful girls who later became their wives. The girls roomed together in a sorority house. After graduation, Johnny became an excellent, highly respected FBI agent and was a wise and caring friend. He had lost his wife two years earlier from a cerebral hemorrhage.

A few hours later, Vance called an administrator at Brookland and asked her to place his name on the waiting list for an apartment in the retirement community. He made it clear from the beginning, however, that he planned to continue to work—that he had not retired.

Vance looked again at a note he wrote himself when Jennifer was dying. He carried the note in his coat pocket. He wrote the following sentences on the back of a laboratory report that had brought more unwelcome information. He had looked at her as he wrote it. She was gradually dying.

> We first said the magic words—I love you—when we were teenagers. We said those words to each other almost daily during the many years we were married. Two months ago, during a brief period when you were lucid, we repeated those words to each other for the last time. After that, I continued to say the words to you, hoping that you could hear me.
>
> You supported my every move, made our house a home, and now you are improving heaven. You deserve the credit for rearing three young men. Being emotionally strong and understanding the grand scheme of things, you told me to *carry on.* I will try to do that, but I cannot conceive of a world without you.
>
> My home life has been a love story—never to be forgotten.

Vance called his three sons to come to Greystone early on April 26, 2004. The four of them circled Jennifer's bed, holding her hands as she died.

Five and one-half months later, Vance moved into Brookland. The home where he and Jennifer had lived so happily for fifty years was sold within forty-eight hours as Vance cried in silence and depression.

Three words kept coming back to Vance. They were, "Jennifer, come back."

CHAPTER 2

October 2004
Brookland Square

Vance's apartment at Brookland Square was right for him. Living alone for five and one-half months in their home on Blackland Road had not been easy. The agony could not be described. Jennifer had predicted that. Vance had lived in three rooms—the den and library, one bedroom with bath, and the kitchen, which included a breakfast room. He never went upstairs where the other bedrooms were located and could not force himself to enter the living room or dining room.

His apartment at Brookland Square had a large central room, which served as a living room and dining area, two bedrooms, two baths, and a small kitchen. Vance's middle son's wife had moved the furniture that was needed from his home on Blackland Road to the apartment. She made it look easy, but such a move required considerable talent. Vance had new bookcases built to house his large library of books, many of which he had written. He planned to use one of the bedrooms as an office. However, the only modern machine he planned to locate there would be a fax machine.

He divided the bookshelves into two parts. He placed a copy of the books he had written in one part and the books related to President Hulgren, his longtime friend and patient, in the other part. The five photographs of the White House that he placed on the wall were given to Vance by Hulgren when he was president. Jennifer's favorite watercolor painting of a dogwood hung above the sofa. The bookcases in the "office room" were filled with books of every variety. A few of the awards that Vance had received were placed on one of the walls.

Vance placed a single picture of Jennifer and him in the "living room area" of the large room. The walls of the bedroom were filled with photographs of Jennifer that had been taken during various stages of their long life together. There was a picture of Jennifer when she was five years old; another one with Vance when they were teenagers; their wedding picture; one with her first grandchild; one with Vance in Athens, Greece; and one taken on St. Simons Island with the entire family on her eightieth birthday. A print of a painting by Gauguin hung above the bed. It was a constant reminder of a wonderful visit Vance and Jennifer made to the lovely French island of Tahiti. Vance studied each of the photographs and the painting each night when he went to bed—hoping to sleep.

Brookland Square is located on famous Peachtree Road. It was one of the first premier retirement communities to be built in Atlanta. The eighteen-story retirement community had led the way. There are numerous such facilities in Atlanta now—one of them is next door, and another one is across the street. Many of Atlanta's well-known business leaders, physicians, and teachers spend their senior years at Brookland Square. Three meals are offered each day, but only two are offered on Sunday. If one chooses, the meals can be brought to the apartment for a small additional fee. Many residents do that. The food is excellent—most of the time. The service is excellent too—most of the time.

The second floor of Brookland is reserved for those who are sick or need extended care. About 10 percent of the residents die each year because many of them have been at the retirement community for ten to twenty years. When a death occurs, a red rose is placed in a vase on a table along with a photograph and a card bearing the resident's name and occupation. The roses are placed where all the Brookland residents can see them as they enter a hall that leads to the dining room. Sometimes there are two roses, and on rare occasions, there are three roses. A sign-up sheet is placed near the photographs of those who died for those who wish to attend the funerals. Transportation is then furnished by Brookland.

There are 180 apartments at Brookland Square and 248 residents. Some of the residents bought two apartments and had them remodeled into one large apartment. There are 57 males averaging eighty-seven years of age, and 191 females, averaging eighty-seven years of age, residing in the community. There are 30 married couples. Some of the residents are in their seventies, and several of them are in their nineties. Two of the residents are over one hundred years of age.

A full day of activities is planned for the residents of Brookland. The plan includes exercise classes, lectures of all types, happy hour, dances, sing-alongs, religious services, movies, new-resident introductions, birthday celebrations, and many other activities. Vance discovered that he could not participate in all the activities as long as he continued to work at Greystone University Hospital. The demand for an apartment at Brookland Square was so great that the board of directors planned to add a large and more modern wing to the building. It is scheduled to be completed in 2008.

Fortunately, Vance already knew many of the residents at Brookland Square. His and Jennifer's interest in the community was initially stimulated because Vance's former partner at Greystone, Dr. Robert Logan, and his wife had moved there several years earlier. He and Logan had been partners for decades. Logan was a famous cardiologist who had opened many doors for Vance, and Vance treasured his friendship and mentoring. Logan understood Vance's great loss because his beautiful wife died a few years earlier. In addition, there were several other well-known doctor friends living there, as there were many of Jennifer's lady friends. Johnny Hendrick, Vance's college roommate, became his mentor. Vance kidded Johnny by saying he was his social secretary.

The waiting list for an apartment at Brookland Square was six months to a year. Life is simpler there because after buying an apartment, a monthly fee takes care of the expense of meals, taxes, lights, heat, water, security, etc. Laundry is billed separately. A valet service for your car is available during certain hours each day except Sundays. The well-trained members of the staff are helpful at every turn. Vance was quick to recognize the ability and professionalism of the staff members who sat at the front desk. They always responded to questions and knew everyone by name.

The social activity at Brookland Square is interesting and somewhat complex. There are four types of happy hour. The first one is large. The *hour* is generally 4:30 PM, and *happy* is created with a bit of alcohol. This type of happy hour is sponsored by Brookland Square, and the community pays for the drinks along with hors d'oeuvres. The second type of happy hour is similar to the first one but is related to a dance. The community pays for the alcohol, chips, and nuts. The third type of happy hour occurs when a resident selects six or seven other residents and asks them to meet in the lounge. The guests bring their own alcohol, and the community pays for the chips and nuts. Vance preferred wine or a soft drink. The various groups dine together at 6:00 PM. The fourth type of happy hour occurs when a resident invites six or seven other residents to his or her apartment. It is to the dismay of some of the women that the gatherings held in various apartments are almost always organized by ladies rather than men. The hors d'oeuvres and drinks are supplied by the hostess. The invited guests meet for happy hour and then sit together for dinner in the dining room at 6:00 PM. A four-course dinner is usually completed by 7:30 PM. Following dinner, the participants go their separate ways to their apartments.

The men at Brookland have varying amounts of white hair. Most of the ladies also have white hair. Their hair is always neat and very much in style. A few ladies dye their hair black or brown. Sometimes it is possible to see a bit of their white or gray hair along each side of the part giving away what they thought was a secret.

Footwear is revealing. It allows Vance to suspect osteoarthritis or gout in some of the residents. Women with arthritis of the joints of the feet wear sandals that sometimes do not match their classy dresses or slacks. Men with arthritis of the joints of the feet wear high-priced tennis shoes, which clash a bit with the swanky suits they wear. The signs of osteoporosis are evident in most of the women.

Men are required to wear a tie and suit to dinner, and women are asked to dress formally. Johnny taught Vance to roll up the end of his tie and tuck it in the inside coat pocket located in the left side of his suit. Johnny even knew how much money he had saved as this act prevented the soiling of his tie with bits of food. Casual wear is permitted during the day at breakfast and lunch. The men try to wear a different suit, shirt, and tie each day. Most of the ladies wear very attractive slack suits most of the time, but a beautiful dress is occasionally seen. Vance kids some of the women who wear slack suits that they wear pajamas and that he had read that dresses are making a comeback.

Many of the residents have macular degeneration. The condition is mild in most of them but is severe in a few. Vance soon learned that some of the residents did not return his hand signal used as a greeting because their poor vision prevented their recognition of him or his signal. Glaucoma and cataracts also plagued several of the residents.

One of the chief complaints of several residents at Brookland was that their physician had asked them to discontinue driving their car because they had fainting spells. Several of them had pacemakers, and many of the residents had abnormal heart rhythm. So in an effort to prevent a stroke, some of them were taking a "blood thinner" because of a heart-rhythm problem.

Vance learned that each resident had many stories to tell. They were all coping in their own way—preparing for the final event of their lives. Some of them complained about being old, but most of them did not. They all disliked the idea of someday having to go to the second floor extended-care community, but they rarely talked about it.

Vance studied the faces and postures of the residents. Some of the more-than-ninety-year-old women were beautiful and carried themselves with the grace of the young. Wrinkled—yes. Stooped a bit—yes. But still beautiful. Several ladies had a rather severe tremor, but only one had Parkinson's disease. A few of the men were athletic in appearance, but most of them had gained weight especially around the waist. The longer they stayed at Brookland, the more likely it was that they would eventually need to use a cane to keep their balance. However, those who participated in the exercise classes remained highly mobile much longer. A few of the men had moderately severe tremors. A few of each sex had very early signs of Alzheimer's disease. Vance was impressed with the spirit of the residents as they each created their own coping methods. Vance noted that the activities offered by Brookland were participated in by residents who planned to remain as active as possible.

Vance learned the names of many of the residents by studying their photographs and names, which were reproduced in a large book located in the well-stocked and superbly organized library.

The residents who ate in the dining room could be categorized as using no cane, those who used a cane, those who used a walker, and those who had a helper push them in a wheelchair.

Vance knew he was depressed. He clearly was not himself. He had returned to work before he moved to

Brookland. He realized that dealing with the brains of young aspiring medical students and house officers would help him cope with his great loss. He recognized that he had a remarkable opportunity to work with excited young people during the day and learn from the wisdom of older people during the late afternoon and night. But he remained depressed.

Vance, being a newcomer to Brookland, could, in the beginning, appreciate only a broad view of the residents who lived there. He noted that they always waved at each other and they spoke to each other. The women clustered together to dine and talk. Women seemed to manage their loneliness and sorrow better than the men. Vance, with a practiced eye, noted that even the women would occasionally pause and develop a faraway look in their eyes as they undoubtedly thought of their past lives and braced themselves for the inevitable events of the future that were certain to come.

Vance looked forward to interacting with the other residents. He wanted to know more about them as individuals with fascinating stories to tell.

Johnny promptly taught Vance two things. Dining etiquette was different at Brookland. A person could leave the dining table without giving a reason while the others were still eating, and a man would be classified as one member of a couple if he ate with the same lady three meals in a row. Vance noted that there were several such couples at Brookland.

Vance usually went to bed at 9:30 PM. He always looked at the pictures of Jennifer that he had placed on the wall, as well as the one taken during a visit to Greece that he had placed on the end table next to the bed. He said, "Jennifer, I need you. Please come back. I want to hold you in my arms."

CHAPTER 3

Early November 2004
Greystone University Hospital and
Brookland Square

Vance was up as usual by 4:00 AM. He showered, shaved and dressed, made and drank his decaf coffee, and read the morning *Atlanta Journal-Constitution*. He walked with difficulty to the elevator and then to the garage. He depended on his cane. There was no valet service at five in the morning. There was no traffic either. Eighteen minutes later, Vance opened the door to the teaching conference room named for him on the fourth floor of Greystone University Hospital.

Greystone University Hospital and Greystone Clinic were known throughout the world. Patients came from within the city, state, country, and from abroad seeking diagnoses and treatment. Vance was pleased that Greystone was consistently listed as being one of the top ten cardiac centers in the country. The university itself, located in beautiful Dewey Hills, had become one of the best-endowed universities in the county.

The medical center, located near the famous Centers for Disease Control, consisted of Greystone University Hospital, Greystone Clinic, a large pediatric hospital, a cancer center, three large research buildings, a school of nursing, a primate center, a geriatric center, and a vaccine center. In addition, the new Greystone-Crawford Long Hospital had just been completed in the middle of Atlanta. Greystone was also affiliated with Grady Memorial Hospital and the Atlanta Veterans Hospital. The facilities were unsurpassed anywhere in the world; and the reputation for patient care, teaching, and research was in the top drawer. Now there were plans to build a new $2-billion Greystone University Hospital and Clinic. Vance reflected on how things were a half century earlier when he joined the full-time faculty at Greystone University School of Medicine. He was more than pleased, as chairman of the Department of Medicine for three decades, that he had been a part of the development of the medical school, its four hospitals, and the Greystone Clinic.

Vance always visited the coronary care unit, where he met with the nurses, interpreted a few electrocardiograms, and enjoyed another cup of decaf coffee. He was proud of the coronary care unit because he had designed it many years earlier. It was the first unit with a wraparound hallway with specifically designed family areas. This arrangement made it unnecessary for family members to go into the center of the unit on their way to visit their loved one; they could enter the room from the outside hallway. This arrangement made it possible for privacy to be maintained.

Vance knew the value of nurses, so he knew and respected them all. He realized that doctors could not take care of sick patients in a hospital without skilled nurses. He also pointed out to all who would listen that the nurses were overworked and underpaid. He worried that schools for nurses were closing and that American women and men were not entering the profession of nursing in sufficient numbers to meet the increasing need. Thank God for the excellent Indian, Korean, Philippine, and Jamaican nurses because they were saving the profession.

Vance visited the nurses' station that was located on the cardiology floor. He asked the nurses if the interns and residents were performing as they should. Was any one of them having trouble? Did the interns and residents answer their calls promptly? Vance learned to value the opinion of seasoned nurses regarding the competence of interns and other house officers. Today they reminisced about a brilliant young intern who responded to an emergency only after several phone calls. When he finally appeared on the floor to see the patient, he was barefooted and was wearing a ball cap. The patient undoubtedly wondered whether he was in a hospital or at a ballpark. Vance recalled the rather long session he had with the intern. It led to the removal of the ball cap and an understanding of the value of shoes. Vance pointed out that there was a place for ball caps and that it was out of line to ask a sick patient to adjust to such an unusual attire for a doctor who was supposed to comfort her. How would he feel if the pilot of an airplane presented himself to the passengers wearing a bathing suit? More importantly, Vance hoped the intern learned that excellent doctoring required more than knowledge of medicine. Vance monitored the subsequent behavior of the intern with the ball cap and no shoes. With a little mentoring, he did fine. He became an excellent doctor.

By 6:45 AM, Vance was sitting in his conference room. The house officers assigned to the cardiology service who had admitted new patients to the hospital during the last twenty-four hours were summarizing their conclusions by writing the Problem List of each of the patients on the whiteboard. Vance assisted them as they struggled to learn how to be clear and brief, but complete. Another faculty member, Dr. Joseph Craine, arrived at 7:00 AM. He was an excellent cardiologist and teacher. He had trained with Vance some twenty-five years earlier. His talent was obvious, so Vance had added him to the faculty. Now prematurely gray-haired, he was a leader at Greystone and one of Vance's treasured friends. All house officers and students assigned to the cardiology service arrived no later than 7:00 AM. During the next hour, the clinical findings of several patients were discussed including the interpretation of electrocardiograms, X-ray films, and other information provided by high-tech procedures. The session was called morning report.

Vance always made a few general remarks when he met with each new group of interns and residents. He usually said, "Welcome to the cardiology service. I intend to teach you cardiology during the next month. My major interest is to assist you in your search for a learning system that you will use on all services during your training. You will also use the system when you leave your teachers to practice or climb the academic ladder. I must tell you, I never met an intern that was skilled. Don't be upset with me because I have made such a statement. Please remember, you were only introduced to skills in medical school—you did not perfect them during your medical school days. That is why we have house staff training. If you were already skilled, you would not need house staff training. We, your teachers, must facilitate your learning and supervise your development as a skilled physician. This, above all else, includes the skill of thinking, which is different from the simple memorization of material. Almost all of my teaching effort will be directed toward helping you solve patients' problems.

"Our time is limited, so here are some questions for you to address. What is the definition of a profession? What is thinking? What is the definition of reading? What is the definition of teaching? What determines if you remember things? What is learning? I will discuss these questions with you as we meet on a daily basis.

"One final thing. Knowing medicine does not automatically make you a doctor. The best doctors always place the patient's comfort and well-being before their own. They care deeply for the welfare of the patient. Please remember that. Now we will start our morning report. I see that Dr. Don Meadows has written the Problem List of the patient on the whiteboard.

"Let's see if Don has been complete but brief. We need to ask Don what information he used to create the problem statements. We need to know if all the abnormalities he discovered are accounted for in his Problem List." Vance proceeded to analyze the work of an obviously brilliant intern.

The intern, Dr. Don Meadows, presented some additional information on the patient. Vance said,

"Don, you did well. Your analysis of the appropriate data was really excellent. I would give you an A on what you have written and said. But let's try for an A+. You say the patient has angina pectoris. Your description of the patient's chest discomfort leads me to agree with you. But you did not state if the angina was stable or unstable. I am sure you know that they are two different conditions, and both are usually, but not always, due to coronary atherosclerosis. They are actually different subsets of the same disease. All of you must understand this because the molecular biology, pathophysiology, the treatment, the prognosis, and subsequent complications differ greatly in the two conditions. If you tell me the angina pectoris began last week—or anytime during the last sixty days—then you must label the angina pectoris as *unstable,* and your treatment plan should be quite different than it would be if you designated the condition as being stable. There must be no change in the angina pectoris for sixty days before you can label it as being stable. When the angina pectoris occurs more frequently, or is produced with less effort, or occurs at rest during the last sixty days, it is labeled as being unstable. Having said all of this and recognizing that you, like all of us, may not remember what someone else says about a subject, I suggest that you read about the difference in stable and unstable angina in this handout and in a textbook and meet me in the morning at six thirty to discuss it."

Vance learned early in his teaching career that a true teacher facilitated the learning process of trainees but should not take it over. Such a teacher always follows up to be certain that important points have been understood and implemented. That is why he planned to meet Don the next morning. Vance added to Don, "This is how you move from A to A+. Please understand, you will learn more when you engage your own brain in your quest for knowledge than you will learn listening to me. My role is to tell you as honestly as I can that this is important and that it is something you must understand."

Don smiled and said, "I understand, and thank you. I will be ready in the morning."

Vance stopped the group at the door of the Vance Connelly Cardiology Teaching Conference Room and said, "Please read the morning paper. Another pharmaceutical house has been caught withholding information about the toxic effects of their latest 'miracle drug.'"

Vance went to his office to prepare for a one o'clock conference on electrocardiography, answer e-mail, review the galley proof for an article he had written for a journal, and polish an article he was preparing, entitled "What Do Good Doctors Try to Do?"

Before leaving the office, Vance called Joseph Craine and said, "Joe, we have a great group of trainees. They will do well."

Joe responded, "I agree."

Vance continued, "Joe, didn't you finish your training about the time Dan Baldwin and Gerald Colfax finished theirs?"

"Yes, I did. They are practicing in Savannah."

Vance responded, "I know. Somehow I have them on my mind. I ran across a picture of them and remembered that I read something in the newspaper about them. If you hear anything, let me know."

"Right."

Vance arrived at his apartment at Brookland at 3:00 PM.

He always checked his mailbox for mail. Today, he received the *New England Journal of Medicine*, a note from a former house officer who was getting married, a few bills, and junk mail. Several other residents were opening their mailboxes, which were arranged by number along the wall of a hallway off from the lobby of the faculty. Some of the residents would sit and sort their mail very carefully. They threw the junk mail into

a large trash can and cradled their personal mail like
it was a newborn baby. The faces of the residents told
the story. Vance could determine the content of their
letters from the look on their faces.

Vance took the elevator to the third floor where his
apartment was located. There was a note on the fax
machine from his friend Johnny Hendrix.

> Please meet me in the lounge at 4:30 PM.
> Max Jenkins, the former president of Aurback
> College, has invited us to happy hour in the
> lounge. There will be six other men and
> women there. Bring your own drink. The
> group will have dinner together afterwards.
> Johnny

Vance sat in his large comfortable chair and
pondered his situation. He realized he was still very
depressed. He felt the need for sleep. So he dozed off
for a brief moment. He then struggled to get up and
walk. His legs were becoming weaker, and he had to use
a pair of pliers to open a bottle of water. The news on
television was not encouraging. The leaders of a large
private company in Houston were in deep trouble.
Government officials were also in deep trouble for
taking bribes. No good news. Vance felt his depression

increasing. But he realized that he should meet and know all the people at Brookland.

The other members of the group were already at a table in the lounge when Vance arrived. After the introductions, Vance asked the waiter Henry for a glass of Sprite. Vance was not prepared to bring wine or any other beverage.

After a few minutes, Max excused himself; bowed to his companion, Belle, who was warm and understanding; and walked across the room to another table where ten ladies were having their own happy hour. He singled out Dolly. She was a beautiful hundred-year-old woman. Max asked her to please play the piano. She did so for the next twenty minutes. Several of the men at Vance's table joined her at the piano and sang. She played several oldies, but her favorite seemed to be "I Love You Truly." When she finished, everyone in the room applauded. The spirit of those who resided at Brookland was becoming clear to Vance. They all loved Dolly. The group left the lounge at 6:00 PM, dined together, and then went quietly to their own apartments by 7:30 PM.

Vance went to bed at 8:30 PM because of increasing fatigue and continuing depression. He marveled at the spirit of those he had met. He thanked God again for the opportunity to be with enthusiastic young people during the day and to be able to tap into the wisdom of the old and very old at night.

Vance looked at the pictures of Jennifer on the wall of his bedroom. He said aloud, "Jennifer, come back. I miss you so." Sleep did not come quickly. Vance's thoughts were of Jennifer.

CHAPTER 4

Late November 2004
Greystone and Brookland

One of the patients at morning report was presented by the intern Dr. Sam Chambers. He was tall and lanky and spoke with a British accent. He wrote, illustrating his excellent penmanship, on the whiteboard that the patient had two problems. One was diabetes mellitus, and the other one was acute shortness of breath. Vance asked him, "What caused the shortness of breath?"

Sam responded, "Pneumonia, heart failure, pulmonary embolism—there are many causes."

"That's right, there are many possible causes. But your patient is not a textbook where all causes of shortness of breath are discussed. You must decide which one of the many causes actually caused the problem in your patient. What did the electrocardiogram show?"

Sam handed Vance the tracing because he had not learned how to interpret electrocardiograms. The computer readout simply stated that the T waves were abnormal. Vance glanced at the tracing and said,

"The tracing shows that your patient had an acute and large heart attack. In addition, his heart rhythm is abnormal. He has atrial fibrillation. This, Sam, reveals how important it is for you to learn how to interpret electrocardiograms. Remember, you can't depend on the computer reading. You are responsible for the interpretation!"

Sam blurted out, "But he had no chest pain—just shortness of breath."

"That is fairly common in patients with diabetes. The nerves to and from the heart are sometimes damaged in diabetics, and the patient may not sense the pain of a heart attack. The patient developed congestion of the lungs and shortness of breath because the heart damage caused the pumping action of the heart to become inadequate. By the way, Sam, I will discuss the electrocardiographic signs of heart attacks at one o'clock today. Each of you must learn to interpret electrocardiograms early in your internship so you can use your knowledge during the remainder of your house staff training. Sam, it's time to catch up."

As the group was leaving, Vance said, "Read the newspaper today. There is a story of a lawsuit against a doctor because he did not diagnose a heart attack in a busy emergency room. Sam, be sure to read the paper."

Vance could not dispel his thoughts of Dan Baldwin and Gerald Colfax. He decided to review the records on the two former trainees. He recalled that something happened during their training that bothered him. What was it?

Vance struggled with the walk from his office to the room where the records were stored. He almost fell but was saved by his cane. He initially thought the door to the record room was locked because he could not open the door. His secretary, Mildred, accompanied him and opened the door with ease. She then located the records and handed them to Vance. She returned to the office while Vance, with paper and pen in hand, reviewed the records of the two former trainees.

Vance opened the file on Dr. Dan Baldwin. He found the form that all candidates fill out when they apply for internship. The letters of recommendation, along with the grades and evaluations of Greystone faculty for his years of house staff training, were also all there.

Dan Baldwin was born in Ogulla, South Carolina, in 1942. He finished high school there in 1960. He completed his college work at the University of South Carolina and graduated from the Medical University of South Carolina in Charleston in 1964 in the middle of his class. His father taught high school in Ogulla. He had one sister and one brother.

Vance had interviewed Baldwin when he applied at Greystone University for internship in internal medicine. Vance remembered the interview. Baldwin was quiet and polite. Vance recalled that he answered questions clearly and used few words to make his point. Baldwin answered most of Vance's questions but occasionally said he did not know the answer. Vance remembered that he was one of the few applicants who did that. Vance liked that. Vance had written in the record, "Let's take him. I believe he is a clear thinker who is not afraid to say he does not know."

The color photograph showed that Baldwin had red hair and a slightly chubby face with a few freckles. He did not wear glasses as many of the applicants did. He, of course, wore a dark suit as did all the other applicants. Vance grinned when he noticed the dark suit. He always wondered why applicants wore dark suits to an interview and then wore everything but a dark suit once they arrived on the scene.

The letters of recommendation that accompanied the application were boring except for one. Vance knew the author of one of the letters. The professor who wrote it was a well-known educator. He wrote, "Baldwin is a good thinker and hard worker. He is not flashy, but he is a solid student. Take him."

So Vance ignored the several long, rambling letters that appeared to be form letters and accepted the suggestion made by the educator who wrote the short note.

Vance felt relieved because he found no clue in the file that would suggest that Baldwin would have a bad experience later in practice. In fact, Vance thought Dr. Dan Baldwin showed many of the characteristics that suggested he was developing into a better-than-average doctor.

Vance wondered, as he read various opinions that had been written by the faculty, if all of them used the same measuring rod to measure the performance of a trainee. Baldwin's notes about patients were brief but complete. Such notes always trumped a long but incomplete and rambling note because it was a sign of clear thinking. Vance was a bit pleased because Baldwin had, he believed, lived up to his expectations during his internship.

Vance opened the file of Dr. Gerald Colfax. He remembered him too. He recalled that he had received a telephone call from an acquaintance affiliated with the University of Texas School of Medicine in Houston stating that Colfax was greatly interested in coming to Greystone as an intern in internal medicine. The acquaintance also sent a letter stating the applicant's interest. A staff member arranged for another professor to interview him but arranged for Vance to meet him for a brief period of time.

Colfax was born in Chicago in 1942. He attended high school there and graduated from the University of Chicago in 1960. He graduated from medical school at Western Reserve in Cleveland in 1964. He did well academically and was in the top 10 percent of his class. He was a member of the honor society. His father was president of a large bank in Chicago. He had no siblings. He had published one scientific paper. Vance remembered the brief interview. He recalled that Colfax came on rather strong. His handshake was slightly painful.

The photograph of Colfax showed him to be rather handsome. His features were clean-cut, but he was beginning to lose his hair—pattern baldness, it was called.

Vance remembered that Colfax moved his chair closer to the desk where Vance was sitting and said, "Dr. Connelly, I really like it here, and I am so pleased to meet with you."

Vance recalled that he said, "I am pleased to have you visit."

Vance remembered what Colfax said: "I will try to answer any question you have. I know positions here are highly competitive."

Vance recalled that he said, "I always have a few questions, but your main interview will be with Dr. Martin. I am sure he will have a few questions for you."

Vance remembered that Colfax persisted. "I don't mind. Go ahead, I will try to answer any questions you might have."

Vance recalled that he asked Colfax a half dozen questions. He quickly responded to all of them, but in half of them, he deviated from the subject. What he said was true, but the answers were not precisely germane to the questions. The answers sounded great but were a bit off the mark. Vance often told trainees that he too went to school and learned how to get a professor off his back by simply saying something that was true in response to a question. As a rule, the professor would give up even though a precise answer to the question had not been given. So Vance often said to trainees, "I will stop you if your answer is true but is not germane to the question." So Vance was a bit troubled when Colfax did not answer the questions in a direct and simple way.

Dr. Martin's interview was clearly summarized. Martin was greatly impressed with the applicant. The letters of recommendations were all excellent.

The faculty at Greystone wrote that Colfax was an outstanding house officer. He read the literature and expressed himself without being asked to do so. He was greatly interested in clinical trials and seemed to excel in statistics. He gave excellent lectures and worked with several faculty members to complete and publish five scientific papers.

Vance recalled an experience he had with Colfax at morning report. Vance was having trouble deciding if a patient had congestive heart failure or noncardiac pulmonary edema. The information provided by Colfax was simply not sufficient to make the differentiation. Vance recalled that he said, "Dr. Colfax, bring us a follow-up tomorrow. I am sure Dr. Adams, who admitted the patient, will be able to decide which of the two possibilities is present."

The next day, when Vance asked Dr. Colfax about the patient, Dr. Colfax did not have a follow-up report.

The following day, Vance asked the same question, and Dr. Colfax responded, "I am no longer on that service, so I don't know."

Such a response troubled Vance; in fact, it irritated him. Vance recalled his response, which was clear to all in attendance: "Dr. Colfax, you don't need to be on the service to pursue the answer to a problem. Since you were the doctor who saw the patient initially, you have the privilege of reading the chart and looking for the answers to your questions. Obviously, you could talk to Dr. Adams. Please remember, the way to learn medicine is to ask yourself questions about your patients and search for the answers. In this case, a simple follow-up would have taught you a lot. Please remember, the alert physician learns from the careful follow-up of his or her patients."

Vance recalled that he wondered if there were two Dr. Colfaxes. One Colfax was presented to others and was always judged as being excellent. The other Colfax was not presented to others but became dominant when no one was looking. The performance of the second Colfax was far less than average.

Vance left the file room with a fresh memory of the two physicians who ended up working together in Savannah. Once again, Vance decided to visit them on his way to his condominium on St. Simons Island.

Vance arrived at Brookland at 3:15 PM. A group of ladies and a few men were filing out of the Brookhaven Room, where a pharmacist had just finished giving a lecture on the value of taking a baby aspirin tablet each day.

Vance asked one of the elderly ladies who had attended the lecture, "What did she teach you?"

The ninety-year-old lady answered, "She said I would live longer if I took a baby aspirin each day."

Vance replied, "That may be correct. Remember, though, aspirin can cause you to bleed from a stomach ulcer. So you must be careful. But what did she say?"

"Oh," she said with a grin, "I have been taking a baby aspirin for years, but I plan to stop if it will make me live longer."

Vance thought about that answer. Her response was interesting. A philosophy that is held by many elderly individuals; they are no longer making a mighty effort to outlive the statistical number that indicated their average survival time.

Dinner with Johnny and Margo was excellent; the soup, salad, fish, beets, sweet potato cornbread, and apple pie were first rate. Vance noted how a table of eight women was animated with talking whereas a table with four men was relatively quiet. Vance was convinced that women can handle the loss of a mate better than men can. Also, they seem to have more to talk about than men do.

Later in his apartment, Vance stood before each of the pictures of Jennifer and said, "Jennifer, please, please, come back." He then hummed the song "How Great Thou Art." It was one of Jennifer's favorites and was one of the songs played at the memorial service for Jennifer. Vance continued, "Jennifer, I can't go on without you."

CHAPTER 5

December 2004
Brookland, Greystone, and the Cherokee Club
Thursday

It was still dark when Vance left Brookland for Greystone at 5:10 AM. No traffic, only three cars.

Morning report was always exciting. He felt he was fortunate because he enjoyed helping the students and house officers with their struggle to get their act together.

Dr. Frank Fitzpatrick, a bright intern who was the son of a former house office, had written the Problem List of one of his newly admitted patients on the whiteboard. Vance thought that the son was very much like the father he had taught some twenty-six years earlier.

Vance said, "Frank, that is a well-thought-out Problem List. A doctor should observe, think, and then state in words the uniqueness of the patient. You have done that with one small exception. You state the patient has an irregular heart rhythm that you labeled as being atrial fibrillation. That is a common rhythm disturbance especially in the elderly. You state the pulse rate was eighty-two beats per minute. It is important to do two things. One, it is more accurate to state the heart rate by listening to the heart with your stethoscope than by counting the pulse. You see, the heart rate may be over a hundred beats per minute, which is excessive, whereas the pulse rate may be eighty-two beats per minute, which is acceptable. Explanation—when there is atrial fibrillation, the weak heartbeats may not be felt at the wrist. Two, with treatment, you must control the heart rate, not the pulse rate. Also, when the condition of the patient permits it, you should be sure that your treatment controls the heart rate, not the pulse rate, after mild exercise."

Vance continued, "You must all read the recent literature about the modern treatment of atrial fibrillation. By the way, Frank, is this patient on the blood thinner Warfarin?"

"Yes, sir."

"I suggest you add that to the Problem List because the physicians who follow this patient must be constantly reminded that the patient is taking that drug. Then, too, it is important for every significant abnormality that is found in a patient to be accounted for on the Problem List. If you measured your patient's prothrombin time, and it is appropriately abnormal, the INR should be on your Problem List. Once again, I say you made an A on your presentation. My comments simply move you to making an A+."

As the group was leaving, Vance added, "Please remember, no doctor is skilled when he or she graduates from medical school. You perfect your skills during your internship and residency and for the rest of your life. So like the musician who asked how to make it to Carnegie Hall, the answer is to practice, practice, practice, and practice. But what you practice must be done well. To practice, practice, and practice anything that is not done well firms up a bad habit."

Vance had increasing trouble getting out of his chair and walking to his office. He was completely dependent on his cane.

His secretary was waiting to tell him, "I just had the strangest phone call from a Dr. Dan Baldwin in Savannah. He said he had trained under you some years ago. He sounded so distressed, I suggested that he talk with you directly. Shall I reach him for you?"

Vance replied, "By all means."

Vance used a special phone that amplified the sounds on the office phone and on the phone in his apartment at Brookland because of his increasing deafness. Mildred signaled that Dr. Baldwin was on the phone.

Vance said, "Hello, Dan. I have been thinking about you and your partner, Gerald Colfax, ever since I saw the piece in the paper about the clinical research that was being done in your private office. How are you?"

Dr. Baldwin answered, "I am physically well, but I do have a problem I want to talk with you about. Will you see me? I want to come to Atlanta to visit you. Could we meet at some quiet place away from Greystone?"

Vance responded, "Of course, we can meet at the Cherokee Club for lunch on a Saturday. What about next Saturday?"

"Fine, fine. I will be there at 11:00 AM.

"That's great. I look forward to seeing you."

"Thank you."

"Good-bye."

"Good-bye."

Vance wondered what could be going on. Why the semisecret meeting?

Vance's 1:00 PM teaching session dealt with auscultation of the heart. He used a computer to test the ability of the group. The CD reproduced the heart sounds and murmurs for virtually all the conditions a trainee was likely to encounter. The trainees were asked to make a diagram that was based on what they heard.

They were rarely able to do that, but after they finished, Vance showed them on the computer screen what they should have heard and diagrammed. He explained, "Excellent auscultation demands that you know what to listen for, that you can hear what you are listening for, and—by identifying the location, loudness, shape, and pitch of the sounds and murmurs—that you can determine the physiological mechanisms that produce them and, from that, can visualize the structural abnormalities that cause the abnormal physiological responses. This act could be called visual thinking. You see, auscultation is not simply hearing something. What you hear should set in motion a series of thoughts. It takes as long to learn auscultation of the heart as it does to learn to play classical music on a piano. So keep listening and thinking until you can do that. Merely hearing something is not the goal."

Vance arrived at Brookland at 3:30 PM. There was a fax from Johnny.

> Meet me in the Brookhaven Room at 4:30.
> Joe Biddy will play the piano for the biweekly
> dance. Johnny

Vance rested in his easy chair for several minutes. He tried to unscrew the cap of a small bottle of water but failed. No strength in his fingers. He gave up and walked slowly to the elevator.

Johnny, who was surrounded by several ladies, motioned for Vance to join him at a table for eight. Vance chose a chair that was next to the wall. He had discovered that the chairs would tend to slip out from under him when he struggled to get up unless the back of the chair was next to a wall.

Brookland supplied the drinks, plus chips and nuts, for this affair, so Vance ordered a small glass of white wine.

Joe Biddy arrived, and the group of thirty to forty elderly people applauded. Although Vance could not dance because of his fear of falling, he enjoyed watching others strut their stuff. What Vance observed was one of the most interesting and inspiring events he had ever witnessed.

Joe Biddy played a certain type of music. Vance, with his hearing deficit, could detect a distinct beat but could not identify the tune of every oldie he played. The audience came alive with action. Ladies, who ordinarily used a cane or walker, would toss them aside and join a partner who had asked them to dance. Vance was astonished.

Vance noted that his friend Tom Jackson, another retired FBI agent, was dancing. Tom was writing a book about his experiences during the time he was an agent. He had severe osteoporosis of the spine, which had forced the trunk of his body to be parallel to the floor. Despite his orthopedic problem, he danced. He had a ball. Vance marveled at his spirit. He admired him greatly.

Jill and Ralph Anderson were at the same table. He was a doctor. He trained at the Massachusetts General Hospital in surgery. He was forced to give up a bright future in surgery because of a severe hip problem. He could not dance, but he would stand, almost without moving, on the dance floor while his energetic wife danced around him. His smart and attractive wife weighed less than half as much as he did. She was graceful and knew all the modern moves. So she danced around him while he remained still. They were wonderful to watch. They were a very interesting couple.

The dance teacher was there, and he made certain that he danced with his former students. He would also dance with the women who were in wheelchairs. He faced them, took their arms, and swung them to the distinct beat of the music. They smiled as if they remembered how it was at an earlier time in their lives.

The group at the table left the dance at 6:00 PM for dinner. They left the dining hall at 7:30 PM and went their own way to their apartments. Alone in his apartment, Vance recounted the events of the day. He wondered what Baldwin wanted to talk about.

Vance then reflected on various stages of his long love affair with his wife, Jennifer, and said aloud, "Jennifer, I loved every stage of our life together. All of them were wonderful, I love you."

Saturday

Saturday was the day of the week that Vance called his day. No Greystone, no Brookland. He usually traveled to Middleton, Georgia, which was one and one-half hours from Atlanta. He grew up in the small town when only five thousand people lived there. There were only a half dozen doctors. Now the town of twenty thousand people and hundreds of doctors was a bedroom for Atlanta. Vance felt comfortable there—a feeling of peace displaced a part of his depression each time he passed his old home place. He visited his last remaining relatives and enjoyed his former classmates including his former medical school roommate. But today he could not go to Middleton because he was scheduled to meet Dr. Dan Baldwin for lunch at the Cherokee Club.

The Cherokee club was considered to be one of the greatest clubs in the nation. Vance had joined the club soon after the club was organized. Back then, the cost of joining was very little. Now the cost was so high he probably could not afford to join. He arrived at 10:45 AM, and Baldwin came through the door at 10:55 AM. Both of them believed it was rude to be late, and Vance remembered that Baldwin was never late at a teaching session during his entire period of house staff training.

"Hello, Dan."

"How are you, Dr. Connelly?"

"Please don't ask because I might tell you. I am hanging in there. I have several health problems, but I continue to work with the house staff and students, just as I always did. They have saved my life. How are you?" Vance noticed that Dr. Baldwin was still thin. He still had a full head of red hair although it was turning white near his ears.

"I am fine. My young grandchildren are fine also. My home life and family are just great."

Vance moved the conversation when he said, "I could tell on the phone that you were troubled about something. I deduce it just to be related to work."

"That's correct. I am sure you remember Gerald Colfax. After we left Greystone, we entered the practice of medicine together in Savannah. In the beginning, we had a great time. We worked hard and tried to use the principles you taught us at Greystone. But things changed about ten years ago. I noticed a great change in the way Dr. Colfax managed his patients. This coincided with the increasing effort the health maintenance organizations made to convert the practice of medicine to a business."

"Go ahead."

"Dr. Connelly, I hope you realize what I am saying to you is not easy for me to say. But I need your help. After all, Gerald is my oldest friend. It's just that I am worried about him, his patients, and last of all, me."

"I understand. Go ahead."

"Well, Gerald began to see more and more patients in order to please the officials at the health maintenance organization. This meant he spent less and less time with patients. I was amazed. Most of the patients did not complain too much because they liked Gerald. Before long, however, some patients were forced to wait an hour or more to see him. Some of them did complain. Then I noticed he was ordering more and more high-tech procedures and listening to patients less and less."

Vance interrupted, "High tech permits us to make diagnoses that we formerly could not make. We could not do modern work without it. The problem is, it is overused, and the value of low tech—the routine exam—is devalued. In addition, young interns believe the reports that are written by people they do not know. They worship the report, forgetting that errors can be made in the interpretation of the procedure. Unfortunately, they may not know enough to challenge the findings printed in the report."

"I know that. But he orders echocardiograms rather than listening to the heart. He orders nuclear tests of the heart on elderly patients with Alzheimer's disease even though the patient has no complaints."

Vance was becoming increasingly concerned about the story Baldwin was relating.

Baldwin continued, "A few years ago, I mustered up the courage to talk to him about my concerns. As usual, he had a quick answer. He said that because the cost of his malpractice insurance was going out the roof, he had to make more money to pay for it. Apparently, he was also getting a kickback from the physicians who performed the high-tech procedures on patients he sent to them. He rightly pointed out that we could not keep the office open with the amount of money Medicare patients brought to the table. He urged me to follow him and organize my practice to make as much money as I could. He said it was impossible to live the good life from the money earned in the new businesslike environment that had closed in on us."

"I can't believe that."

"It is true, sir. But that is not why I have come for help. A few years ago, Gerald decided to add a new dimension to our office. He wanted to do research. I thought that sounded interesting, and I listened to his plan because he had done very little research before. I wondered what he was planning to do, especially if he wanted me to join him. He said that a pharmaceutical outfit named MediSurge had approached him about participating in a clinical trial for hypertension. He also said the company would write the protocol and pay $200 for each patient that he enrolled in the study. The company would have its own experts write the scientific papers that would be submitted for publication but would list him as the author. He was proud of that. He pointed out that hypertension was common in Savannah and that the study could be implemented by a technician who would be paid by MediSurge. This could be, he said, the source of a great deal of money because the company would pay him a substantial salary for organizing and supervising the trial. He mentioned that he would be paid $100,000 annually."

Vance muttered through his amazement, "He was good in statistics, but what you are describing is not research."

"I turned him down. I was thankful that we only shared the same office and that we shared personnel but did not intermingle the finances of the office."

"Well, what happened?"

"Over the next few years, he enrolled several hundred patients in the study. Newspaper stories were written about his civic interest in finding the best treatment for a common serious health problem. He became the pride of the community. He was invited to give talks at all the civic clubs. He was silently making a great deal of money, but that is not what worried me."

"What, pray tell me? What did worry you, if that was not enough?"

"I have copies of three of the forms that the technician filled out on three of their patients. I came across one of the forms because one of Colfax's patients became ill while he and his wife were on vacation in Italy last year. My secretary was told by the patient to look up her record in the research file because I might need it to determine what her current problem might be. Please note that the patient's record states that I referred her to the research study. But I had never seen her before. Note that the records on the other two patients state that I referred the patients to the study. I don't know those patients at all. I wonder if there are such patients. One of the patients lives at

826 Chestnut Road on St. Simons Island. The third patient may also be fictitious—note that his address is Middleton, Georgia. His address is 32 Pecan Avenue. I wonder if there is a street by that name. Maybe she spends the winter in Savannah or St. Simons."

"I understand your concern. I am mortified. Surely, there is an acceptable explanation. I will visit 826 Chestnut Road on St. Simons when I go down there in a few weeks. I grew up in Middleton and will check out that name and address also."

"Sir, I will be forced to leave our office for two reasons. One, I can't cope with this new form of *so-called* medical care, and I am not interested in that type of research. Please help me."

"Dan, I will try to help. Give me some time to think this through. Maybe I will pay you both a visit when I go to my condominium on St. Simons Island in a few weeks. Also, after I think about it, I will call you at home in a few days to advise you what you should do to further strengthen your case that all is not well in the research project. Please, may I keep the copies of the forms that were filled out on the three research patients?"

"Certainly, here are the copies, and thank you."

"I will be in touch."

They parted company, and Vance returned to Brookland. What a disturbing lunch. What should he do? Vance realized it was none of his business. What went on in their office was beyond his reach. But a devoted former trainee was asking for help; and now that he knew about the problem, he felt, for the sake of the profession, he had to do something.

Johnny had sent a fax to Vance's office machine at Brookland.

> Tommy Brown and his wife, Sarah, have asked us to eat dinner with them tonight. See you in the Lobby at 5:30.
>
> Johnny

Vance was pleased. Tommy Brown was a very smart man. He had been one of the top executives at Coca-Cola; and his wife, Sarah, was an accomplished artist. They were a joy to be with.

The conversation at dinner was enlightening. It ranged from politics to business. Vance asked, "Sarah, when can I see your paintings?"

She replied, "How about now?"

Johnny and Vance accompanied Tommy and Sarah to their very large apartment. They had combined two apartments to make a large roomy home that was large enough to house Sarah's studio and paintings. Sarah was currently painting a commissioned piece.

Their apartment was filled with splendid artwork. Sarah's large paintings of single flowers were simply magnificent. As Vance viewed Sarah's paintings, he said, "Move over, Georgia O'Keefe."

Vance entered his apartment at 8:00 PM. He sat on the side of the bed and viewed the photographs of Jennifer on the wall. How could that perfect woman leave him? As depression took over, he called out for her. "Jennifer, help me. I need you."

CHAPTER 6

April 26, 2005
Greystone and Brookland

Going to Greystone at 5:10 AM was not easy because Vance had only one thought all day. It was of Jennifer. Jennifer died one year ago. His middle son planned to pick him up at Brookland at 4:00 PM and take him to the cemetery.

As he hobbled into Greystone, he was greeted by the night crew who cleaned and waxed the floor. Vance brightened up a bit because he enjoyed chatting with everyone who had anything to do with making Greystone a great hospital. He unlocked the door to the conference room that had been named for him and arranged the chairs in a semicircle facing the board. Vance insisted that most lectures were a waste of time. He realized that the value of a lecture depended, for the most part, on how much the listener used the information after the lecture was over. He favored small groups and insisted on one-on-one teaching when possible. He liked to engage the brains of those who were there to learn.

Dr. Jeff Hawking, an intern, had written the Problem List of the patient that he had admitted on the board for discussion. Dr. Craine surveyed the list and made some cogent remarks. Vance's contribution dealt with the interpretation and use of the electrocardiograms that had been recorded on the patient.

Vance said, "The computer readout on this tracing is wrong. Please remember that the computer interpretation of electrocardiograms is wrong about 20 percent of the time. *You* must be able to interpret the electrocardiogram. In this forty-year-old woman, the tracing shows pre-excitation of the ventricles. At times, this abnormality can be mistaken for a heart attack. Patients with this type of tracing may have episodes of rapid heart rate that requires treatment. When this occurs, it is called the Wolff-Parkinson-White syndrome. I know this patient was admitted because of chest pain. We must be very careful here. Just because we know that preexcitation can produce a tracing that looks like a heart attack, we must not assume that the patient does not have a heart attack. Stated another way, the presence of preexcitation does not prevent heart attacks. Her story of chest pain is not at all characteristic of a heart attack. It is more suggestive of gastroesophageal reflux. A nuclear test for coronary disease will be adequate here."

"Yes, that is our plan."

As the group was leaving the room, Vance said, "Remember, the most common procedure performed by internists is the recording of an electrocardiogram. As you know, the electrocardiogram has become increasingly important during the last decade because the diagnosis and treatment of a heart attack and rhythm disturbances are often dependent upon the proper interpretation of the tracing. Meet me here at 1:00 PM. We will discuss the matter then."

Vance added, "The morning paper has a story that should interest you. One of the drug houses paid doctors to prescribe their expensive drugs. One doctor made a fortune. This all came to light because the drug caused heart attacks. How corrupt can doctors get? I have faith in you—you would not do that."

Vance was met at the door of his office by his secretary, who said, "Guess what? We just had another call from Savannah."

"I told Dr. Baldwin I would be in touch with him after I had time to think about the situation. I guess he is wondering when I will call."

"No, no. This call was not from him. It was from Dr. Colfax. They are in the same office, are they not?"

"Yes, I wonder if Gerald knows that Dan came to see me." Vance realized that he must be careful and say nothing to Gerald about Dan's visit.

"Shall I put the call through?"

"Yes, Mildred, of course."

"Hello, Gerald. Glad to hear from you."

Dr. Colfax came through loud and clear as always. "I am just fine. I am so excited about the research I am doing here in the office that I wanted to tell you about it. I will be in Atlanta next Wednesday, and I would like to have lunch with you there at Greystone. Is that possible?"

Vance responded, "That's wonderful. Please come to my office at 11:30 AM, and we will go to lunch."

"Be there. That's next Wednesday."

"Good-bye."

"Good-bye."

Vance shook his head. He felt himself being pulled into a ring of fire. Obviously, neither of the two physicians knew that the other had contacted him. Even more worrisome was the belief that Colfax was trying to suck Vance into the study that he called research. If Baldwin was correct, the work was corrupted. On the other hand, Vance realized that he had heard only one side of the story. He also pondered how he could extricate himself from the entire affair. Why should he be involved? he thought. He was almost eighty-four years of age—life should be simpler.

Vance was scheduled to participate in the twelve o'clock conference for the entire house staff and all the students assigned to the medical service at Greystone. The plan was for the chief resident in medicine to present four or five very brief clinical stories and ask Vance to predict what the autopsy revealed. Vance usually started his analysis by interpreting the electrocardiogram. Dr. Jacobs, a superb cardiac pathologist, would then show slides of the heart that revealed the answer to the clinical problem. Vance always learned a great deal at that conference.

Vance often said at the beginning of the conferences, "We have been doing this for years, and as I am sure you know, I am not always right. Intellectually, I know I can't always be right, and I try to take my misses in stride. But I don't like to miss. I punish myself the rest of the day. I ask myself how I went wrong. I ask myself questions about the case, I try to learn from being wrong. Occasionally, I am rewarded in my arguments with Dr. Jacobs about his opinion. Sometimes he later writes me a note confessing that what I had said about the case was correct. The lesson is you and I must study all of our lives."

When Vance completed his one o'clock conference on electrocardiography, he returned to Brookland. He asked the valet to park his car because every muscle in his body felt weak.

He always talked with the young men who parked his car. Today Joseph was there. Vance asked, "Joseph, how many days each week do you go to Georgia State University?"

"Three, sir. Why do you ask?"

"I am proud of you. You must finish college."

"I know. I know—and I will."

Vance thought that he would do well because he clearly liked people and enjoyed pleasing those he served.

Vance picked up his mail and then took the elevator to the third floor where his apartment was located.

Johnny had sent a fax.

Meet me in the lounge at 4:30 PM for the sing-along. Joe Biddy will play. Johnny

Johnny always met Vance at four thirty, which was thirty minutes early, in order to get a table. He had invited Judith, Margo, Jerry, and Mary. Joe Biddy played the piano while Marilin, the waiter, served drinks, chips, and nuts. The group sang along with Joe Biddy's music. Many of the women knew every song. Vance could not discern the tune but could hear the music. They all asked why he could hear the music but could not identify the tune. He tried to explain why the music was loud but the tune escaped him, but he was unable to sustain the interest of those who asked the question.

After dinner at 7:00 PM, the members of the group went to each of their apartments. Sometimes—in fact, most of the time—the members of a group would leave the dinner table without saying good night or making any comment whatsoever. This was part of Brookland's "rules" and "habits."

As Vance entered his apartment, he muttered, "Jennifer, I can't go on without you."

CHAPTER 7

Early May 2005
Greystone and Brookland

Vance was up early—three o'clock. He could not sleep. He napped thirty minutes at a time and then became wide awake for the next thirty minutes. He was still depressed and was terribly concerned about Colfax's visit at noon. He prepared some prepackaged apple-flavored spicy oatmeal and decaf coffee. Decaf because he had occasional bouts of atrial fibrillation and was concerned that regular coffee, with its caffeine, might precipitate an episode. In his case, atrial fibrillation was caused by the faulty function of the sinus node in his heart caused, perhaps, by the aging process itself. That little piece of remarkable tissue is normally responsible for creating the normal heart rhythm. When it defaults in its duties, the heartbeat originates in the atrium, or where the pulmonary veins enter the left atrium, where it is less well organized. In his particular case, a cardiac pacemaker had solved the problem. Vance was not alone—several others at

Brookland had pacemakers for various heart rhythm problems.

Vance was a nut about his decaf coffee. He used a coffee bean smasher, not a grinder. A grinder, he had been told by another coffee lover, burned the coffee. His friends, knowing of his coffee addiction, gave him excellent coffee beans from Martinez—who was Atlanta's gift to the coffee world. The ritual of the coffee making took longer than using preground coffee, but Vance was addicted to the entire process. No cream. No sugar. Smooth—*mmm*, good.

Dr. Joe Craine was not at morning report. Regrettably, like many faculty members today, administrative duties interfered with his academic duties. Dr. Craine usually discussed the details of treatment while Vance emphasized the minute details of history taking, physical examination, and the interpretation of electrocardiograms and chest X-ray films. Vance believed that good thinking could be taught, so he spent most of his allotted time teaching the interns how to analyze data and how to think.

Today Vance was responsible for the entire conference.

Dr. Terry Adams, a slow-talking, somewhat-frightened tall thin intern, had written on the whiteboard that his twenty-eight-year-old patient had a stroke—along with several other problems. Vance was not happy with his Problem List. He pointed out, "Years ago, it was acceptable to diagnose that a patient simply had a stroke. Today you must determine *why* the patient had a stroke. Was it caused by a thrombus in an artery in the brain, a cerebral hemorrhage, or an embolus? For example, in this twenty-eight-year-old woman, you should consider the possibility of a cerebral embolus. If that is a likely possibility, where did it originate? Did she have atrial fibrillation? Does she have mitral valve disease? Does she have endocarditis? These conditions are common and may be responsible for a stroke due to an embolus. We must determine if she has a patent foramen ovale in the heart that is large enough to permit a small clot to travel from the leg veins to the right side of the heart, cross the little opening in the upper septum of the heart, and pass on to the brain. An echocardiogram is needed. We must look specifically for a patent foramen ovale and for vegetations on the mitral and aortic valves. Please report to the group tomorrow what the attending physician thinks about the cause of the stroke and tell us what the echo revealed. Let us hope that there is a patent foramen ovale because if there is, the defect can be closed using a catheter to place an umbrella-like structure over the hole. Surgery is not needed."

This case enabled Vance to emphasize one of the principles of medicine that he insisted trainees learn. He stated, "Please remember, ask *why* something has happened. You must determine the cause of an event—you do not simply identify that an event has occurred. I sometimes think that college and medical school destroy common sense by forcing students to memorize, memorize, and memorize. A person with little schooling always asks, *why* did a two-car collision occur? Send that person to college and medical school, and he or she may not ask *why* something happens. "

Vance placed his arm around Terry, who was looking a bit dejected. His mother had trained with Vance. Vance said, "You know, I love the house staff. Everyone does not learn the same things at the same time. You are not alone. I have to explain the importance of asking *why* to every group of interns. So look up the cause of strokes in young people, and I will call on you tomorrow to report on the patient and what you have read. Please remember, this is the way you learn."

Vance walked with difficulty to his office. He confessed to himself that he was having more and more trouble walking. He answered mail, reviewed manuscripts for a peer-review journal, talked on his special phone to several faculty members, and tried to prepare himself emotionally for the lunch he was to have with Dr. Gerald Colfax.

Colfax arrived at Vance's office at eleven o'clock. Mildred talked with him briefly and then ushered him into Vance's office.

Colfax was quick to say, "Dr. Connelly, how are you?"

Vance answered, "I am fine, but there are a few things wrong with the body I live in. Thank God, my brain seems to be OK."

Vance noted that Colfax had lost most of his hair and sported a small mustache and goatee. Vance detested both of them. Colfax's suit and tie were obviously from Brooks Brothers, and his shoes were polished like a mirror. Vance also noted that he looked much older, but his aggressiveness had not been tempered by the passage of time.

Colfax hurried on to say, "Thank God you are still teaching. I see in my mail that Dr. Gregory, the current chairman of the Department of Medicine, named the educational program for you. That's wonderful. I will contribute to the Vance Connelly Residency fund."

"Great. I want to tell you, as I tell all former house officers that trained with me, that Gregory is probably the best chairman of the Department of Medicine in the country. He is capable of doing everything—patient care, teaching, and research. He is a giver. You remember I divide people into two groups—givers and takers—he is a giver. Unfortunately, he is tied up with too much administration, as are all modern chairmen. I was lucky when I was chairman, we did not have much money, so my administrative duties did not dominate my activity. I was able to be on the wards of the hospital with the patients, students, and house staff."

Colfax hurried on, "That you were. I am so excited about the research we are doing in our office. I want to tell you about it and solicit your help."

The last few words of that bit of conversation troubled Vance. The words rang loudly in Vance's ears. Vance said, "Let's go to the dining room and find a table that is relatively private."

"Fine, you lead the way."

"Sorry, I walk too slowly to lead, but we will get there."

They chose their food and sat in a rather secluded area of the doctors' dining room. It was early, so there were few others there.

"Well, Gerald, tell me what you are doing in research." Vance silently questioned if he knew the difference in a study that was organized by a biased pharmaceutical company and real research.

"I just love research. You will recall that I was interested in statistics when I was here."

"I do remember." Vance wondered if he really meant that he loved the money paid by the pharmaceutical house to do a study.

"Well, it occurred to me that a practicing doctor should engage in research that involved his or her private patients. As you know, clinical trials are needed to determine the value of new drugs. The patients utilized in clinical trials are often attended by private doctors who refer their patients to doctors who are located in academic centers in order to have them participate in the trials. I reasoned that the private doctors did not need to do that because well-trained practicing doctors should be able to conduct the trial in their private offices."

"I see, go ahead." Vance wanted to hear his pitch but had already concluded that he would not become involved in any scheme that Colfax offered.

"So I asked a pharmaceutical company if I could be responsible for a clinical trial to determine if a new drug was useful in the treatment of high blood pressure. The CEO of the company jumped at the opportunity. The study is extremely well funded, and its implementation has been very interesting and emotionally rewarding. The patients like it, and I feel I am making a small contribution to the profession of medicine."

"I saw the piece in the paper about it."

"Yes, all is well except for two things. One is I can't get my associate, Dan Baldwin, to participate in the research. He, for some reason, won't work with me on the project. He says he does not know anything about research. I can teach him. It is actually very easy. You see, I need his patients in order to reach the predetermined number of patients required to attain the appropriate statistical power."

Vance played it cool and asked, "Why won't he participate? He is smart—he learns easily." Vance silently thought that Dan was a very smart guy indeed to reject Colfax's offer to join him.

"I don't know, but I am worried about him. You know he is my best friend, and I would do anything for him. But he is having trouble changing with the times." Colfax shifted his eyes in a most unbecoming way. "He orders fewer high-tech procedures than I do. He spends too much time with patients at a time in the history of medicine when we must cut the time spent with each patient so we can see more patients in a day. If we don't do that we can't make a living because HMOs and Medicare pay so little for talking time. As you know, you can make more money performing high-tech procedures."

Vance just listened; he was learning a lot from the rapid chatter of Colfax. Money, money, money was entering the conversation more and more, and a caring attitude was hardly discernable.

Vance said, "You mentioned that you had two problems. What is the other one?"

"I need your help. I would like for you to be a consultant on the research project. It will take up very little of your time. Your name would greatly strengthen the final manuscript that will be prepared for publication by the drug house. You won't even have to worry about that—they have excellent writers and grammarians who are skilled at producing excellent manuscripts. Speck MediSurge would pay you quite well, and it would not take up much of your time. Yes indeed, that pharmaceutical company can fix you for life."

"Oh my, Gerald, that is very kind of you, but I am eighty-five years old. I am trying to let my plane down as easy as possible, and it is already overloaded. My plate is full. I just don't see how I can take on any more activities." In addition, Vance knew all about Speck MediSurge because he had dealt with the company earlier. In fact, he had contributed to the company's downfall. He did not know that the company had been rejuvenated. He certainly would not become involved with that company, or any other company for that matter.

"I understand. Please don't say no now. Let me invite you to visit us on your way to your place on St. Simons Island. Also, let me leave a copy of the research protocol for you to review. Maybe your plate will be less full in a few months, and I will hope you can see your way clear to join me."

"Thank you for thinking of me. Perhaps I could visit you and Baldwin in a few months."

They parted company. Dr. Colfax returned to Savannah, and Vance decided to go to Brookland.

There was no fax from Johnny, so Vance napped for a half hour. He thought about the strange statements Gerald Colfax had made at lunch. He also thought about the statements he and others had made in the records of Dan and Gerald during and after their internship and residency. Were there clues in their past records that would have predicted the current behavior of the two men? Colfax was a shrewd operator who had crossed the ethical line. Baldwin was also shrewd but had chosen not to step over the line. Vance decided to read the research protocol, but not with the same purpose Colfax had hoped for. Vance wanted to determine if the study plan was scientifically correct. Vance suspected that Colfax was telling representatives of Speck MediSurge that he, Vance, was in their pocket. On the other hand, what was the truth? The two former trainees gave very different views regarding what was going on. Vance concluded that he was involved whether he liked it or not.

Being exhausted, Vance ordered dinner to his room and went to bed at 9:00 PM. As always, he looked at the pictures on the wall. He choked up and said, "Jennifer, can't you see how much I need you? I want to have dinner with you—no one but you. I want to just be with you."

CHAPTER 8

June 2005
Chicago and Savannah

Hortense Montague barked at her secretary, "Get that fast-talking Dr. Gerald Colfax in Savannah on the phone. He thinks he is so smart. I will, in due time, show him how dumb he is. He can't even land Vance Connelly for us."

Hortense, who was tall and dark skinned, used bright red lipstick. She had broad shoulders and straight black hair. Her pantsuit was the latest. Her high-heeled shoes made her more than attractive. Her broad shoulders forced a listener to listen to every word she uttered. Despite her good looks, she, as the CEO and owner of Speck MediSurge, scared the wits out of everyone who worked for her. Speck MediSurge created drugs and medical devices; the company was recently involved in a class action lawsuit regarding the loss of lives caused by a drug that the company had produced. Deaths and other serious side effects of the drug had been hidden by the company, but the drug had been prescribed by innocent doctors after it was known by the company to be toxic. The company lost the lawsuit.

Speck had sold the company many years earlier to Triplett, who had Mafia connections. Triplett created the so-called modern Speck MediSurge. He was eventually indicted and convicted for a murder he had committed many years earlier. Vance had played a role in identifying him as the murderer of a patient who had been pushed from a window at Greystone University Hospital. Triplett was later murdered by a member of the Mafia. Hortense Montague, who was high up in the administration staff of Speck MediSurge, was waiting for her chance to charge. So, like a leopard, she raised the money to buy the company and, having done so, appointed herself CEO.

As soon as Colfax was on the line, Hortense asked in a sarcastic tone, "I am calling to find out how you are coming along with your research."

Dr. Colfax replied, "It's going well, Hortense. I also contacted Dr. Vance Connelly as you suggested and felt him out about joining us as a consultant." Colfax then lied, "I feel sure we've got him."

"Good. We must have his name on the final manuscript. I don't give a damn if he does any work or not. In fact, the less he looks into the situation, the better. Everyone has his or her price, so land him."

"Don't worry. We will get him. I will convince him."

"Good. Tell him he will be paid $200,000 for his initial consultation fee and a monthly income he can't turn down. If you land him, you will receive $20,000 extra this year."

"Great. You are so generous. I just love working for you."

"Also, offer the doctor who shares your office $50,000 to join up with us. He would get the same fee that you do for every patient he enrolls in the study. We need his patients to complete the study and feed the information to the FDA for approval. I am already working on that. The positive decision by the FDA is already in the bag. That was easy to arrange—the guy in charge at the FDA was a pushover. A little money made him see the value of our drug before he saw the data from the clinical trial. One other thing: be absolutely sure the assistant who helps you is paid handsomely. I have known of cases where an assistant decides to spill the beans because they were not paid adequately. So watch her. Pay her well. Remember, everyone has their price."

"She is OK. She is amazed how much money she can make doing research. We don't have to worry about her," replied Dr. Colfax.

CHAPTER 9

August 2005
Greystone and Brookland

There was much to learn at morning report. Dr. Janet Howell, an attractive red-headed young woman, presented three patients. She was obviously competent, and, equally important, she obviously enjoyed her work. The discussion of one of the patients consumed most of the time. The patient was a fifty-five-year-old man who was admitted to Greystone because of severe chest pain. Dr. Howell was not certain what caused the patient's pain. She also had heard a high-pitched heart murmur in diastole that she believed was caused by aortic valve regurgitation.

Vance said, "Let me ask you a few questions. Was the pain that was felt by the patient located beneath his sternum, and was it maximally severe at its onset?"

"Yes, I believe so."

Vance asked, "Was the pain felt in the back—between the shoulder blades—was it more severe there than it was beneath the sternum?"

"Yes, yes it was."

"Was the blood pressure normal?"

"No, the blood pressure was elevated in the right arm but below normal in the left arm."

"Did the patient have good femoral artery pulses? Did he complain of weakness of the legs?"

"The femoral pulses were barely felt, and he did complain of weakness in his legs."

Vance pointed out, "All of these clues point with certainty to dissection of the aorta. In this case, the tear in the aorta began in the first part—the root—of the aorta and involved most of the aorta. Medication to control the blood pressure is urgent, and he should be seen by the cardiovascular surgeons as soon as possible. Now I suggest that each of you look up and read about this catastrophic disease that we call aortic dissection and be *prepared* to discuss it tomorrow."

True teachers, Vance believed, encouraged trainees to read about the diseases they found in their patients. He learned early in his career that trainees remembered what they read more often than they remembered what he or anyone else said. So he insisted that trainees asked themselves questions and looked them up. Self-learning, he called it.

As the group left the room, Vance asked, "Did all of you read the article in the *New York Times* describing how some physicians were treating patients in a midwestern hospital? Apparently, as the group made ward rounds, the senior attending physician in charge removed the bedcover, pulled up the gown of a female patient, and discussed the characteristics of a surgical scar made when she was operated on for breast cancer. She lay there totally exposed. All of that was done without the patient knowing who the crude examiners were—there had been no introductions, and there was no discussion with the patient. Apparently, no one in the group even spoke to the patient. That is not doctoring—that is not acceptable—that must never occur. The responsible doctor should be fired. Please, please, remember to be kind and thoughtful. The welfare, including the emotional feelings, of the patient must always be placed first."

It was Wednesday, so Vance went by his office, and then went to another hospital that was owned by Greystone. It was a new and magnificent building named for Long, the Georgia doctor who first used ether as an anesthetic. Of course, that claim was challenged by the physicians in Massachusetts, who claimed that Morton demonstrated the use of ether as an anesthetic agent to a group of doctors before Long did. Vance's conference there was preceded by lunch with the chief resident in medicine. He enjoyed the one-on-one conversation that ensued. The food was always delicious. Vance could not resist the fruit cobbler, which made him break his diet.

Vance's conference there with the medical residents was always exciting. Vance tried to predict the diagnosis from a detailed analysis of the electrocardiogram. This was his trademark. He then reviewed the chest X-ray film, information found on physical examination, and the patient's medical history. He then put all the clues together and gave his final opinion regarding the cardiac diagnosis. Vance called it working backward. This, he pointed out, forced one to think more carefully about the findings collected by each method of examination. Today the patient had a heart attack because of exposure to carbon monoxide gas inhalation from a faulty furnace.

Before leaving the hospital, Mildred, Vance's secretary, called. She reported to Vance, "We have a call from Dr. Colfax in Savannah. He has invited you to visit his office. You select the time. What shall I tell him?"

Vance groaned; it was like old-fashioned flypaper. He could not rid himself of the albatross. He said, "I will think about it and will call him tomorrow."

The phone was ringing when Vance entered his apartment at Brookland. It was Johnny. He said, "I can't meet with you tonight for dinner. I am not feeling well, and my daughter, who is a nurse, is picking me up in a few minutes. Good-bye."

Vance sensed that Johnny was in trouble and went to Johnny's room, but there was no one there. Johnny's illness was the talk of the dining room. Everyone wanted to know what had happened to him.

Vance went to the dining room alone. On the way, he noticed the red rose standing by the picture of the resident who had died. She was eighty-eight years old and had lived on the second floor in the extended care unit for two years. Five friends had signed up to go to her funeral.

Vance ate dinner at a table where only two could sit. No one joined him, so he had a chance to study those who were eating in a group. He was interested in a group of six ladies who were seated nearby. When one of the ladies spoke, she leaned forward, and the other five ladies did likewise. As they did so, each of them became wide eyed. They also turned their heads slightly as if they had trouble hearing. She was the leader with a story; they listened, and when she was through, they leaned back in their chairs. This happened over and over. Their actions reminded Vance of the opening and closing of a flower, if such could happen.

When Vance returned to his apartment after dinner, there was a fax from Johnny's daughter stating,

Dad had a small thrombotic stroke and
is having trouble moving his right leg. The
neurologist says he is doing well and will
probably recover with little residual damage.

Vance passed the good word to a large number of
interested and caring people at Brookland.

Vance stood before one of Jennifer's pictures, kissed
it gently, and said to himself, "I miss you so." He kissed
it again and, with her on his mind, tried to sleep.

CHAPTER 10

Early September 2005
St. Simons Island, Savannah,
Brookland, Cherokee Club, and Middleton
Thursday

Vance decided to spend a few days in his condominium on St. Simons Island before visiting his former trainees in Savannah. He would see them on the way back to Atlanta on Friday. This way, he would have time to think before setting foot in what he believed to be a corrupt situation.

He and Jennifer had purchased the condominium in Ship Watch some twenty-five years earlier. They loved the place, the ocean, the pool, the town, the food, and their friends. Vance knew the trip to the island would be emotionally difficult for him because Jennifer's touch would be everywhere, even in the restaurants where he would eat. She and he loved Chelsea, the Crab Trap, Crab Daddy, Mullet Bay, Barbara Jene, the 4th of May, Blanch's (until it closed), Delaney's, the Red Barn, the Georgia Grill, and the King and Prince.

They used to dine at the Cloister, but a few years ago the management of the first-class resort clamped down. If you did not stay at the Cloister, which was located on Sea Island, another nearby island, you could not dine there.

Vance pretended that Jennifer was with him as he did the things she liked to do. She walked the beach while he sat and watched her. He loved watching her. Vance continued to have sleepless nights—he felt he could not go on without her. He tried to write. He tried to look at television. He tried to walk by the sea. He tried.

Vance spent five days on the island and then traveled to Savannah on Friday to see his former trainees. He knew what he had to do. His search for Chestnut Road on St. Simons Island had convinced him. He had checked out the patient's address that was listed on the form supplied him by Dan Baldwin. There was no such street on St. Simons Island. He checked new and old telephone books—there was no person whose name matched the name that was listed on the research form filled out by Colfax. This meant that Colfax was making up names and addresses of nonexistent patients in order to meet the requirements of the research project. Vance decided to reserve his final opinion about the matter until he checked out the existence of the person and the street Colfax had listed as being in Vance's hometown of Middleton. But Vance could not help but think that he was becoming more and more deeply involved in a very corrupt enterprise.

Friday

Vance drove his Avalon from St. Simons to Savannah rather quickly on the expressway. He planned to step into their office reception room and sit there for a while—observing and listening. He told the receptionist that he knew he was early and hoped he could sit there for a while and rest before she actually announced his arrival. She looked at his cane and agreed.

Vance overheard one elderly woman who was waiting tell a man to her left that she had been waiting to see Dr. Colfax for over an hour. But she said, "It is worth it because he is not only a doctor, he is also a scientist doing very significant research. I do wish he would spend more time with me like he used to do."

The other waiting patient said, "Well, I see Dr. Baldwin. He talks to me. He even called me one night to discuss the results of my lab work. He is almost always on time, but the word around is that he may be leaving. I hope not. I depend on him. But he says he can't continue to make a living if the current Medicare pay system continues. He says he can't afford the malpractice insurance. He can't send his kids to college on the money he makes. He loves medicine but feels he can no longer deliver what he wants to deliver. He tells me it is getting to be impossible to know what the truth is about the drugs and devices that are currently being produced. That bothers him a lot."

Vance was hearing what he suspected. The spirit of good doctoring was dying in Dan Baldwin, and the shift of emphasis from humanism to the abnormal love for tainted money had gained a strong hold on Gerald Colfax. *How very sad,* he thought.

A very attractive neatly dressed young woman came up to Vance and said, "I am Dr. Colfax's assistant. I help him with his research. He and Dr. Baldwin would like for you to join them in his office."

"Thank you, Ms.—?"

"My name is Agnes. Agnes Hightower. I am so glad to meet you. Both doctors speak of you often. They say very nice things. Come this way."

Colfax's office was large and elegant. A medium-sized side room served as a dining area. The table was set for lunch. The three of them were seated as directed by Dr. Colfax. They were served crab Louis, fruit, lime pie, and sweet tea.

Vance was astonished. He did not realize that such food was served in doctors' offices. Vance noted that Dan Baldwin ate very little and said nothing while Gerald Colfax talked a great deal but was able to eat all the food with no problem.

Dr. Colfax said, "Dr. Connelly, you can't imagine how honored we are to have you visit us."

Vance replied, "I am pleased to be here, and I thank you for the delicious lunch."

"I am eager to show you our research area. I do hope you will see why it would be to your advantage to join us."

Dan Baldwin spoke for the first time, "Dr. Connelly, you have inspired us all to place our patients first, so I must go see some patients. Like you, I do not wish to keep them waiting. Thank you for coming by."

With that, Baldwin left.

Ms. Hightower joined them as they moved to an area that was designated as the research area. The patients who were in the study were seen in that area of the facility. It was there that Ms. Hightower talked with them, recorded their blood pressure, and drew blood for examination. The furniture was top notch. Much better than in Vance's apartment at Brookland. They were able to see ten patients in the area at the time.

Ms. Hightower said, "We see about ten patients every two hours. As you know, they are paid by the pharmaceutical house to be in the study. Therefore, the patients like to participate. Here is the type of record we keep on each patient."

Vance reviewed the form as if he had never seen one like it before. He remembered that some of the entries were made up by someone. The false entries must have been made by either Ms. Hightower or Dr. Colfax because no one else in the office would be likely to make entries on the form.

Dr. Colfax, who had been called away to answer the phone, said on his return, "I just checked with my boss, Ms. Hortense Montague, and I have a surprise for you, Dr. Connelly, but I will spring it on you a little later."

Vance said, "Let's see, it's two o'clock. I must get on the road. It takes me six hours to drive to Atlanta, and I want to be at Brookland by eight o'clock tonight.

Colfax said, "I will escort you to your car."

As Vance was getting into the car, Colfax said, "I checked with my boss in Chicago to be sure I was doing what she wanted. That was the phone call that I made during your tour of the facilities. She advises me to offer you $200,000 for your initial consultation fee and $100,000 per year to join us in the research project. It would take very little of your time. No more than an hour each week."

Vance acted surprised, but he was not surprised. He looked Colfax straight in the eyes and said firmly, "That is a generous offer, but you know I would not feel comfortable taking money and doing very little work for it. I hope you understand."

Colfax read Vance's eyes. He knew for sure that Vance would not be joining him. Colfax also sensed that Vance saw straight through him.

The trip back to Atlanta was uneventful. He arrived at Brookland at 8:14 PM. His Brookland friends had completed dinner and were in their apartments. Shortly after he sat down in his easy chair, the phone rang.

"Hello. This is the Connelly apartment."

"This is Ms. Hightower in Savannah."

"Yes, Ms. Hightower."

"I want to talk to you—I must talk to you alone—somewhere. Where and when can we meet?"

"Can't you write me a letter?"

"No, I want to talk, not write."

"All right. Meet me at the Cherokee Club on West Paces Ferry on Sunday at 11:30 AM. This is Friday. Can you find an excuse to come to Atlanta Sunday?" Vance carefully guarded Saturdays—that was his day, and he intended to go to Middleton.

"I will be there. Good-bye."

Vance looked at the pictures of Jennifer and said, "Can't you see, I need your help. Please come back. I want you to hold my hand."

Saturday

Saturday was Vance's day—no Brookland during the day and no Greystone. Saturday was designated as the day he usually went to Middleton. Sunday was designated as the day Vance's three sons and their wives came to Brookland to see him, so Vance always left the late afternoon open for them.

Vance was up by four o'clock, polishing a scientific manuscript that would be included in a book about heart disease.

Vance left Brookland in his Avalon at 8:30 AM, traveled west over a bumpy road to the expressway that carried him to the road that entered Middleton on its eastern side. The one-and-one-half-hour trip seemed short to Vance. This trip to Middleton was not Vance's usual pleasure trip. This particular trip was being made because Vance wanted to check on Pete Miland, who allegedly lived on 32 Pecan Avenue. The name and address had been listed on one of the forms Colfax had filled out and sent to MediSurge. Dan Baldwin had given Vance the form when he visited Vance a few months earlier. Vance questioned if such a person or street existed. He suspected that they were both figments of Colfax's imagination.

A feeling of contentment always replaced his black-dog depression as he entered the city limits of Middleton. He drove by the house where he grew up. He relived his youth for a few seconds. He could name the people who once lived in the houses on the entire street when he lived there.

He noticed that expressways were everywhere, and there was a circumferential highway as well. What a change. Little business buildings were everywhere in the outskirts of the town. There were traffic lights and bank buildings everywhere. His old high school building, which was designed by the famous architect Neil Reid, still stood but was used for something else. A new and larger school building had been built somewhere. Vance mused that he doubted if the teachers were better because as the years passed, he marveled at the quality and number of the teachers that guided him during those important early school days. He passed where the Middleton Clinic and Hospital used to be. He and a friend, Donny, had spent hours at the small facility where some of the doctors had their offices. There were about eight hospital beds in the building.

There were only a half dozen doctors in the little town. Now there were hundreds of doctors and a large three-hundred-bed hospital. Medical specialists of all types were currently located in Middleton. There were many orthopedic surgeons, cardiologists, neurologists, dermatologists—you name it, the specialists were there. The medical center drew patients from a thirty-five-to forty-mile radius.

He passed the beautiful courthouse. It had not changed. Vance had happy memories of the courthouse because when he was a young teenager, he would sit quietly on the back row of the courtroom and listen to all types of trials. He was intrigued by the skill of the lawyers. He learned the difference between direct and circumstantial evidence, which is used in the profession of medicine as well as in law.

He noticed that the tall statue of a Confederate soldier was now located at the courthouse; it had formerly been located in the middle of the town square. Vance drove slowly into the area that was called the square. In his youth, there was a large central area with marble seats on each of the four sides of a grassed area. The tall statue of the Confederate soldier stood majestically in the center. Most of the buildings in the town were arranged to create the four sides of the square. Access to the square was provided by roads that entered the area in the middle of each of the four sides. Vance identified the department store building where he worked each Saturday from 7:00 AM to 11:00 PM for $1. Seven decades ago, the town and the marble benches were filled with farmers who came to town on Saturday. As the nation grew, the buses and trucks became so large that they could not circle the square area that held the Confederate soldier. Since this occurred before the superhighways were built to accommodate such large vehicles, the mayor decided to eliminate the central structure and move the statue. When that was accomplished, the beauty of the square was changed. Then as time passed, large—very large—shopping centers were built in the enlarging suburbs of the growing town. And as the country changed, there were fewer and fewer farmers to fill the town on Saturday. The buildings forming the square were there, but the purpose they served was very different now. There were many eating places like the Corner Café, the Warehouse, Pearls, Miller's, the Irish Pub, Alley Cat, Mea Bella, McGee's Bakery, and Pirelli. There were two coffee shops—one of them was associated with a hundred-year-old bookstore. There were numerous places to eat in the suburbs, whereas in his youth, Vance was brought up on the food at the Greenfront, a small place that was located away from the square near the railroad station. Back then there was only one other place to eat—a restaurant near the square, but few people went there.

The second story of many of the buildings was now used for lofts.

Earlier there was one four-story bank building "on the square." Vance noted that the building was now only two stories high. Apparently, when the building, which housed the only elevator in town, was renovated, the upper two stories were in such bad shape the owners decided to remove them. Vance hated that because his father's office suite was located on the fourth floor. Vance's memory flashed back to the past: his father spent the first half of his life as a teacher and school principal. Because during and after the Depression he found he could not support his family on $90 a month, he changed his profession. He was one of the first to develop the Federal Savings and Loan Association, a program created by President Franklin Roosevelt to fight the Great Depression and to assist anyone who wanted to own his or her own home. Many of the homes in Middleton and surrounding areas were financed by the Middleton Federal Savings and Loan.

Leaving the square and going west, Vance saw the new Cultural Center that had recently been added to the growing town. Plays, concerts, and art shows were now available. When Vance was growing up, a graduation play might be shown in the auditorium at the Fire Station. Moving on westward, Vance noted the numerous small business buildings with more places to eat. He saw, to his astonishment, a huge liquor store. He thought, If that building had been built when he was growing up, the people involved would be kicked out of the church, and the place would have been boycotted.

Vance slowed his car to fifteen miles per hour. He was approaching the university. He drove into the front road of the university and parked his car near the building where Jennifer had stayed when she attended the school. He saw the tree where he first held her hand and told her that he loved her. She, thank God, returned his love. This strangely did not deepen Vance's depression—if anything, it strengthened him and diminished his grief. He and Jennifer had attended the school for two years in the earlier days before it became a four-year school. He then transferred, as did Jennifer, to the university in Athens, Georgia. He recalled how marvelous the teachers were at the small school. He remembered too that his participation in several plays helped cure his shyness. There were only 150 students in the freshmen and sophomore classes. The smallness of the classes was a great positive asset.

Vance appreciated that more and more as he himself became more involved with medical teaching. Now there were ten thousand students. The school is now a thriving university with dozens of buildings and plans for the future.

To the left was beautiful Sunset Hills. There was an excellent golf course and a magnificent country club. Beautiful and expensive homes were built on spacious plots of land all around the golf course. One would think the houses in *Gone with the Wind* had returned. None of that was dreamed of when Vance was growing up.

Vance simply let his car wander into many of the new areas that were being developed. There were numerous new streets filled with houses equal to those on the most fashionable streets of Atlanta. The suburbs in all directions were filled with huge shopping centers and eating places.

When Vance was a teenager, there were only a few millionaires in the town. He remembered the rumor was that they had to pay income tax, but no one else made enough to be taxed. It was in this context that Vance heard the word *tax* for the first time. Now it seemed that there were hundreds of millionaires in the town-city. They, the millionaires, were generous. They contributed to the development of the town.

Many of them were developers who recognized that Middleton was becoming a bedroom of Atlanta. Vance was astounded to learn about a new development that was under way. Plans had been made to add a total of more than thirty thousand new homes within a few miles of Middleton. This would, within ten to twenty years, add ninety to a hundred thousand new people to the area.

Vance turned his thinker on. He concluded that there were two reasons why the thriving town was changing so rapidly. One was that a friend of his had developed a method of manufacturing wire. The business thrived and became the planet's source of wire. His friend, Dick, and his wonderful widow, Annette, loved Middleton and not only created a great source of jobs but gave generously to the civic needs of the town. This included support for the hospital. The other reason the town was on its way to becoming a city was the development of the university into a superb place of learning.

Vance enjoyed being with his classmates. He felt so close to them. He sat side by side with many of them for seven years—five years in high school and two years at the two-year college before it became a university. He was also meeting many new friends now. Vance was a frequent guest at their monthly supper club. New friends were there as well as former classmates and two former medical students. Vance especially enjoyed the Saturday pancake breakfast. The pancake breakfast was offered for $6 on each of the four Saturdays in the month of February. Kroger grocery store gave the flour, bacon, and coffee; and members of the Kiwanis Club did the cooking. The whole town showed up! They would serve about one thousand people each of the four Saturdays. It was held at the restaurant the Mansion. They collected the money for the breakfast and divided it between fourteen charity organizations. The restaurant had been the home of the man who owned the textile mill some seventy years ago. Vance also attended the annual Magnolia Ball that supported the hospital. The proceeds amounted to about $450,000. Currently, the money was being spent to modernize the portion of the hospital that was devoted to cardiology. He had been invited, along with one of his classmates, to the ball each of the last two years by Annette, the widow of the founder of the Wire Company, to join her at the $10,000 table. The ball was held at her beautiful estate near the buildings that created the world-famous wire. Vance thought about how, when he was growing up in Middleton, there probably was not a tuxedo in the town. No one could afford a $10,000 table, whereas now there were sixty-seven such tables at the ball. He thought too how much easier it was to get around, dine, and be entertained in Middleton than it was in Atlanta. When he attended the late-night affairs in Middleton, he stayed at a bed-and-breakfast that was owned and operated by the mother and the father of the owner of the Mansion.

Vance studied a new map of the area. There was no street by the name of Pecan Avenue. He checked the telephone book and did not find the name *Pete Miland.*

Vance had lunch with his medical school roommate, Donny Shepard, and returned to Brookland a few hours later. Donny was a smart, hardworking student and doctor who had given his professional life to Middleton. Donny had never heard of the name *Miland.*

He freshened up in his apartment and joined a group of nine others for happy hour in the lounge at 5:00 PM. The former president of a university and his companion, Belle, were the hosts. After that, they dined together. As they walked the hall from the dining room to the lobby, Vance saw a red rose. He read that Mr. Maciano had died. Vance and the others were stunned. That quiet and distinguished Italian was loved and respected by everyone. He had been a high official in the Coca Cola Company—successfully leading the corporate giant in London, France, Italy, and the United States. But Vance knew that was not his real passion. He was an accomplished sculptor. He made huge abstract structures that were the talk of the art world. When Vance talked with him, he exuded great pleasure when he discussed his large pieces of abstract art. He did not talk about the soft drink industry. Everyone at Brookland bowed their heads to acknowledge the death of this remarkable man. Vance knew, as did everyone else at Brookland, that they too would be a red rose someday. The role of each of the residents was to cope with the end of life in a dignified and loving way.

Vance looked at the pictures of Jennifer that surrounded him in his bedroom. He said, "Jennifer, I wish you had been with me today. That little town and school we used to know are no longer there. In a few more years, the town will be a part of Atlanta. I want you to know that I felt your presence when I looked at the large oak tree where we first said we loved each other."

Sunday

Ms. Hightower arrived at the Cherokee Club at exactly 11:30 AM. The maître d' showed them to their table.

Vance began, "Ms. Hightower, I am pleased to see you. I detect you have something on your mind that could not be written and could not wait."

"That's right, sir," Ms. Hightower replied.

"They have a delicious Sunday buffet. Now I must ask you for a little help. As you can see, I am deaf—note the large hearing aids. But don't talk too loud please. You simply speak distinctly and face me so I can read your lips. If I don't understand, you can write your message to me in this little notebook. Also, although I hate to ask you, will you please help me carry my dishes of food back to our table? You see, my right hand is occupied with a cane, and I always worry that I can't support a plate of food with my left hand."

"Oh, of course, I will be glad to help."

When they returned to their table, Vance said, "Go ahead. I am all ears—hearing aids and all."

"I hope you have perceived that I am an honest person. I am in over my head. I can't go on without your help. I am party to a sham operation. I want out." She wiped a tear from her cheek and gave a little sob.

"Wait a minute. Slow down. What do you mean?"

Vance knew what she was about to tell him, but he played it all with a straight face.

"Dr. Colfax is making a fortune with his research program. He pays me a lot of money to help. In fact, he recently doubled my salary. But I can't go on. I have noticed that there are more filled-out forms than there are patients. He is making up patients. They don't exist. Also, I have seen him change some of the blood pressure recordings without actually measuring the blood pressure. He seems to know which patients receive the new drug and which patients receive the placebo. The records are all in favor of the new drug. Side effects are minimized by eliminating some of the complaints. You see, he fills out the final forms, and my notes, which are accurate, are shredded.

"On top of that, he tries to make love to me. He offers me fabulous amounts of money to sleep with him. I refuse to do so. Once he tried to force his way on me. He said he and his wife had split and that they would be divorced soon. He can't fire me because he knows that I know too much. But I can't go on. What can I do?"

Vance sensed that the entire operation was coming to an end. Baldwin was leaving the practice because of the corrupt research operation, and Ms. Hightower was about to sing to somebody.

Vance said, "Ms. Hightower, I am not surprised. I sensed all that you have told me and have real evidence for some of it. We are both in the same boat. I hold information that is similar to yours. I believe we must go to the prosecuting attorney in your area and ask him for advice and help. You realize, I am sure, that we are getting deeper and deeper into a scandal that will rock the whole nation."

"Yes, I understand."

"Then I suggest you see the prosecuting attorney in your area as quickly as possible. I will talk with him also after you locate him and talk with him. Please call me—give me his name and phone number."

"I will do that Monday."

"Now enjoy your midday feast."

They parted at 2:00 PM. Vance was not happy, but he had predicted what Ms. Hightower was going to tell him. Vance had attended church Sunday morning. He had given the church a new grand piano in honor of Jennifer. The music that came from the piano was beautiful, but it always made Vance sad. Vance left Sunday afternoon unscheduled because his three sons and their wives usually visited him and brought him up-to-date news about his six grandchildren and three great-grandchildren. Today was no exception. Vance was very proud of his three sons and their wives. They brought Jennifer to life each time they visited.

There was a note under the door from Margo, who was Johnny's close friend. Johnny was much better. He had slight weakness of the right leg and would go to a rehab center on the Greystone campus for a few days.

Vance was alone in his apartment as the night came. He stood before each picture of Jennifer. Each one brought back specific memories. Vance said, "I love you. I will join you before too long."

CHAPTER 11

Savannah
Sunday Night

Agnes Hightower traveled by taxi to the ever-busy Hartsfield-Jackson airport in Atlanta. She arrived just in time to catch a 3:30 PM plane to Savannah. She landed in Savannah without a problem and rushed to her car. She drove frantically to her apartment, which was located in one of Savannah's nicest suburbs. The time was 6:32 PM.

Agnes was dog-tired. Her problem was destroying her. She had never faced such a problem and viewed her situation as hopeless. She sat in a large chair in her living room, kicked off her shoes, got up, and walked to the refrigerator and selected a bottle of Chardonnay. She sat down again and sipped a glass of wine every thirty minutes until 8:05 PM.

She decided to take a warm bath. Maybe that might help her sleep. As she undressed, she looked in a full-length mirror and thought, *Not bad for a forty-eight-year-old single girl. Must be the wine*, she concluded. She grasped a straw when she recounted her session with Vance Connelly. He now shared her problem with her. That was helpful. Also, she knew what to do next. She would call the local prosecuting attorney tomorrow.

She adjusted the temperature of the water and filled the tub. Just as she did so, she heard a metallic-like clink. She turned to look but heard no more. She shrugged her shoulders and stepped into the warm water. She slid her body down so that she was covered with warm water. Only her head was above the water. She thought, "God gave us this wonderful, relaxing, warm water.

She felt much better—maybe she would survive. Then it happened. She felt a strong hand on each of her shoulders. The hands were pushing her head under the water. She got a glimpse of a huge man with a silk stocking over his head. He looked horrible—his facial features were completely ironed out by the stocking except for his hideous eyes and mouth. She struggled, but his strength was the greatest she had ever known. She knew she was being murdered, and in a flash, she knew why.

The man removed the silk stocking from his head and went to the living room. He sat in the easy chair and poured himself a glass of wine. He savored the wine and was at peace with the world.

He decided to move her body from the apartment. He would wait until midnight when the streets would be silent. Another glass of wine.

He searched the apartment for a swimsuit. He found one, and holding it in his hand, he enjoyed another glass of wine. He then pulled the swimsuit up and onto Agnes. He found a raincoat for her to wear on the little trip he planned for her.

He cleaned up the bathroom. He drained the tub. No one could ever guess that she had taken a recent bath.

When midnight arrived, he placed the almost-empty wine bottle in the refrigerator, surveyed the scene, and placed her on his shoulder. He arranged for her to be in the sitting position in the passenger seat of the car. He forced her head back—adjusted the angle of the back part of the seat—so that she looked as though she was sleeping.

He traveled to an isolated spot on the Tybee Beach. He pulled off his clothes except for his underpants. He removed her coat and carried her to the edge of the water. He waited a moment until the tide came in and, as it receded, swam with her some two hundred yards into the ocean. There he left her.

He felt satisfied that he had completed a very professional job. His colleagues in Chicago would be proud of him. Then he mumbled out loud, "Now, Hortense, bitch that you are, broad-shouldered witch, I will call you at your office tomorrow and demand that you pay me twice the amount of money we agreed on. After all, I spent more than four hours working on this job. It's worth at least ten grand."

CHAPTER 12

Late September 2005
Chicago and Brookland
Monday

Hortense dialed Dr. Colfax's number. She was in her more-than-swanky Chicago apartment. She sat on the side of her bed because she was angry as only she could be. It was early—seven thirty, Monday morning. Her hair was a mess. No lipstick. No false breasts. Ugly toenails. She crossed her right leg over her left and repeatedly kicked her right leg while smoke from her cigarette swirled around her head. Without her false shoulders, she would not impress anyone. The way she dialed signified her great unhappiness at the moment. She was calling Dr. Colfax on his home phone in Savannah. "Dr. Colfax, this is Hortense at MediSurge. Do you know where your assistant, Ms. Hightower, was yesterday? I am sure you don't! You incompetent jerk."

Colfax responded with a trembling voice, "No, Hortense, I do not. Why should I?" He recognized

Hortense's anger and felt a surge of adrenaline. He also felt a wave of nausea as his palms became wet with sweat.

"Does it surprise you that she had lunch with Dr. Vance Connelly in Atlanta on Sunday? I am amazed that you are so dumb. Here I am, hundreds of miles away from Atlanta, and I know more than you do about the people who work for you."

"Yes, it does surprise me. She had just seen him here on Thursday. What's going on?" His voice quivered because he realized that Hortense could wipe him out if she chose to do so. He sensed that she was angry enough to do just that.

"Do you have any idea what they might talk about? Oh, I am sure you don't, you innocent little squirt. Why, oh why did I ever get hooked up with you?"

"No, I do not."

"Well, I do, you moron. I am sure she told him that the records you have sent me on your research patients have been altered and that some of the patients do not exist. You are not even a good deceiver. I believe she spilled the beans to Connelly. Now she and that old doctor will tell somebody—I don't know who—but they will talk. And you, sir, will be accused publicly of being a small-time stupid crook."

"Oh my god." With that comment, he almost fainted.

"You had better take care of it as soon as possible, or your ass will be on a hot plate pronto. Understand? What a jackass you are!" She yelled again, "You understand?"

Colfax regained a bit of his usual composure and said, "Hortense, if I am in trouble, you and MediSurge are in bigger trouble."

Hortense paused and shouted to him, "You fool! You dumb idiot. You don't understand. I and MediSurge will accuse you of falsifying data. All I have to do is tell the court that I did not tell you to do that." With that, she slammed her phone down.

Colfax was pale—his hand trembled as he dropped the receiver back into its cradle. He grabbed his face with both hands and groaned out loud.

Tuesday

Vance was up at 3:30 AM. He rode his stationary bicycle for thirty minutes, showered, shaved, and prepared his morning coffee and oatmeal. At 4:30 AM, he retrieved his *Atlanta Journal-Constitution* from the mailbox located outside of his apartment door. He cringed as he read the news:

> Ms. Agnes Hightower, a respected medical research assistant, was found dead

in the ocean near Tybee Beach. She was
apparently swimming in the area late Sunday
afternoon, and despite the fact that she was an
accomplished swimmer, she succumbed to the
undertow that is known to be severe in that area.

Vance shivered as he read it. He knew she was
murdered. Now he was the only one who knew the
whole story and realized that he too could be murdered
because he knew too much.

Vance left his apartment at Brookland at 5:15 AM.
He knew he would have to struggle to keep his mind
focused on teaching the house staff because the news
from Savannah was alarming and serious. On the
other hand, teaching medicine was his life and usually
trumped any annoying distractions.

The young lady intern was an Indian, as were many
of the interns, nurses, and cardiology trainees. Vance
was greatly impressed with the ability, work ethic, and
devotion the Indians, Lebanese, and Vietnamese had
for excellent medicine. As with the other Indians,
her handwriting and English were excellent. In fact,
they spoke more perfect English than the native-born
Americans. She had prepared a superb Problem List
that revealed the complete medical and emotional
status of her patient.

Vance simply congratulated her and made the following remarks to the entire group, "My job is to find out what you know and don't know. If you know something, we will not discuss it. If you don't know something but should know it, we will discuss it together until you do know and understand it. You, of course, should debate with me about the need for you to know something. If I can't defend the need for you to know something, then we won't discuss it. This is the way to focus on what really matters. Dr. Patel, I can see that you understand your patient's problems. Accordingly, there is no need to discuss them further.

"May I point out to the group once again that it is highly likely that your previous schooling required that you memorize, memorize, and memorize. That method of teaching kills your curiosity and destroys your passion to think. In fact, many trainees become addicted to memorizing but have great difficulty using the information they memorize. I am more interested in what you do with the information you memorize than I am in how many facts you can recall. Remember, thinking is the rearrangement of information into a new perception. Remember too that learning implies that you have used the information in a thought process, or performed an act until you are fluent. That means you practice, practice, practice until the act is done easily and quickly."

As the group was leaving, Vance added, "More and more articles are appearing in lay journals stating that some medical schools are offering special courses on caring for patients. The schools are alarmed about the displacement of caring by technology and wish to emphasize the continuing need for doctors to care for their patients. I have always believed that a young person learns to care for their fellowman from their mother and father. I once proposed that all mothers should have LOVE written on their kneecaps so that young toddlers would be made aware of caring at a very young age. I agree with the schools and programs that set up a system where caring is emphasized as much as technology, but I also believe that they must be very careful. Smart young people can memorize a playacting type of caring that may not be real. I want each of you to have the real thing. Care for your patients, and they will be more likely to follow your instructions, be less depressed, and be happier. It is the honest thing to do. Then, too, caring leads good doctors to study and remain competent."

Vance went quickly to his office. He had an urgent telephone call to make. He had to talk with Colfax in Savannah. He would simply say to Colfax that he was sorry to learn about the accident. He called and asked to speak with Dr. Colfax. He was told that Dr. Colfax had gone to Mexico for a short vacation. Vance then asked to speak to Dr. Baldwin. He was told that Dr. Baldwin was no longer there. He had left the practice.

Vance, now alone with his information, had to decide what to do with it and how to protect his own life as well.

Vance had dinner with Johnny; Margo; Susan, who was the very competent president of the homeowners association; and her husband, Jed. Vance noted that everyone was looking at the new lady who just entered the dining room. She wore a large red hat. None of the other ladies ever wore hats in the dining room. The newcomer also wore a red jacket over her black pantsuit.

Susan pointed out, "I met her. I talked with her. She is very nice and creative. She makes some of her own hats and some of her dresses. She has one hundred hats and loves to wear them. In fact, she always wears one. She has white hats, black hats, purple hats, red hats, blue hats, green hats, orange hats, every color of hat. They look good with her brunette hair. She is a very interesting lady."

The new resident wore the hat with dignity and pride. Although the other ladies did not wear hats, they admired the attractive brunette from Mitchell County.

Johnny asked, "Vance, are you going to the dance Thursday night?"

Vance replied, "No. I love to watch you all, but my legs won't let me dance. I would fall all over the lady. Also, I can hear the music but can't determine the tune because of my deafness. I have decided it's best not to worry you people with my presence."

Johnny said, "It's no problem, but I understand. Well, anyway, did I tell you about the lady that did fall? This happened before you moved in. She fell and could not get up. The paramedics were called, but before they arrived, someone pulled the tablecloth off one of the tables and draped it over her. The music continued and couples continued to dance around her lying there on the floor. This continued until the paramedics removed her."

Vance thought, Only at Brookland. He loved the spirit of the people as they squeezed the last pleasures out of the diminishing number of days that were left for them.

Leaving the dining room, the residents passed the table where the red roses are placed. There was one tonight. The man was over one hundred years old, a former professor at Georgia Tech. He once told Vance, who asked him why he was moving to the second floor, that "no one who is one hundred years old should be alone. I will have more company and help in the extended care community."

Vance always felt lonely when he closed the door of his apartment. He reread the paper. He reflected on the urgent vacation that Colfax had taken. He wondered if Colfax had killed Agnes. His so-called vacation in Mexico suggested just that.

"Jennifer," Vance said, "I am in real trouble. I know too much. I need you. Please help me. You have never failed me. I love you."

Chapter 13

Early October 2005
Brookland

Vance had been a resident at Brookland for one year. Brookland was preparing a special dinner for those who were born during the month of October. That included Vance and his former partner, Robert Logan. Vance would be eighty-five years old. He was scheduled to sit with Jan, who was the widow of one of Vance's associates at Greystone. The theme for the night was *Casablanca*. The décor fit the night, and two of the ladies played the parts of Humphrey Bogart and Ingrid Bergman. The lady who assumed the role of Bogart wore a trench coat and hat and a pantsuit. Vance did not recognize who she really was. She made a very good Bogart. Vance was astounded because attractive exotic dancers were recruited for the entertainment. The eighty- to ninety-five-year-old ladies and gentlemen applauded the dancers over and over. Surely, each member of the audience silently wished they could do all that the dancers did.

The dinner was outstanding and was enjoyed by all. Once again, Vance was impressed by the people at Brookland. They had learned to carry on—even with many emotional and physical burdens that were unknown to others. They cared deeply for each other while recognizing that they too would eventually be reduced to a single red rose and would be remembered only briefly.

Vance had a number of problems, but none was more urgent than his proper disposal of his Savannah information. He must seek legal help in Atlanta. Healthwise, at eighty-five, Vance believed his brain was intact; but he was depressed. He missed Jennifer more than words could tell. His hearing was continuing to decline, and despite exercise, muscle weakness overpowered him. He held Jennifer's picture in his hands and said, "I love you."

CHAPTER 14

Mid-October 2005
Brookland and Greystone

Vance woke up at 1:00 AM thinking about a lawyer. He must retain a lawyer. His morning bran muffin and decaf coffee from Martinez were consumed without him tasting them. His mind was on his information problem. So he sat in his specially designated thinking chair and thought it all through.

The ride to Greystone was hardly remembered because Vance's mind was on the plans he had conceived in his thinking chair. Morning report was rewarding because Vance was continuing to learn medicine. An attractive young Lebanese woman presented the Problem List on the first patient. She wrote beautifully and spoke clear and precise English. As written, her young female patient had pericarditis. Vance asked her, "What data did you collect from the patient that permitted you to make that diagnosis?"

She replied, "Three definite clues were present. One, the patient had precordial pain that was worse on inspiration and relieved by shallow breathing. Two, I heard a definite three-component pericardial friction rub. Three, the electocardiogram shows generalized epicardial injury. The ST segment vector is directed toward the cardiac apex."

"Very good. Do you have any questions about your patient?"

"Yes, we must determine what caused the pericarditis. She had a febrile illness a few days prior to the chest pain, and we are assuming the condition is viral in origin. But we must follow up and look for lupus and other serious causes."

"Very good again." Vance snapped out of his depression and worry. He admired her statements—all of them were clear, germane, and simple. Vance knew that she knew how to learn, was curious, asked the question why, and could communicate with precision. She had made his day. He knew she would do well. She did not need a teacher.

Vance reminded the group of interns and residents not to use abbreviations in their written reports of patients. Abbreviations can lead to errors.

Vance went to his office, determined to find a lawyer. He called his friend, the former president of Greystone University, and asked his advice. What a great thinker. Vance trusted him completely. He advised Vance to retain Attorney James C. Smith, who graduated from Greystone school of law. Vance thanked him, and the former president wished him well.

Vance called the office of Mr. Smith and made an appointment to see him the following Wednesday at 3:00 PM. Vance finished up in the office at 3:00 PM and beat the traffic to Brookland.

Vance and Johnny chose a four-chair table in the dining room. They were soon joined by Delda and Beth. Delda traveled everywhere. She was agile and smart. Vance had taught her daughter in medical school. Beth was the widow of a well-known and popular politician. She was attractive and managed her macular degeneration skillfully. She and many others at Brookland had outlived their eyes, but they carried on bravely. They would say, "What else can you do but carry on?"

There was another red rose standing stately on the table. Vance noted the sheet of paper where names are placed by those who wish to ride in a bus to the memorial service. There was only one name. Vance thought about that. He understood that the longer you lived, the smaller the number of people who would attend your funeral.

Vance said good night to Jennifer's pictures at 10:00 PM. Those pictures were the last thing he saw at night and the first thing he saw in the morning. She was with him always.

CHAPTER 15

Mid-October 2005
Brookland, Greystone, and Midtown Atlanta
Wednesday

Vance slept until 4:30 AM. That was unusual for him. Perhaps because he had developed a definite plan of action, he was able to sleep longer. Six and one-half hours of sleep was a lot for Vance.

Dr. Craine was especially good today at morning report. Vance recognized Craine's ability many years ago when he was in training and enticed him to join the faculty. His discussion of the treatment of the patient admitted at 3:00 AM could not have been improved upon. Vance was pleased that Craine had been awarded the Vance Connelly Professionship in Cardiology.

Vance congratulated the intern Dr. Arran Campbell, who presented the patient. He added, "I note in the chart that the patient had an automobile accident several years ago. Apparently, she was thrown forward even though she had fastened her seat belt. I wish to make two points. The type of accident and the date should be listed in the Problem List. Remember, the patient's Problem List should include current problems and all significant past problems. The word *significant* as used here means that any problems that influence the patient's current or future health should be listed on the Problem List. The list should also include a listing of the absence of all preventive measures such as the absence of a lipid profile as well as a list of the inactive problems such as past surgical procedures.

"When the severe accident is listed on the Problem List, it reminds the physician to check the chest X-ray film carefully since a traumatic aortic aneurysm might show up some years later.

"An excellent complete Problem List is the trademark of an excellent physician. Such a list reveals the uniqueness of the patient and the expertise of the physician who created it."

As the group was leaving, Vance said, "Don't forget, look up something on every patient. When you link new information to a patient you are responsible for, you will remember what you have looked up. That's the way to learn medicine."

Vance worked in his office until 11:00 AM. He then had lunch with the chief resident at Greystone Crawford Long Hospital, and taught the house staff there at his twelve o'clock conference.

Vance arrived at James Smith's office at 2:45 PM. Smith belonged to a group of lawyers. They had all graduated from Greystone law school. They were all well known and were considered to be Atlanta's best.

"Welcome, Dr. Connelly."

"How are you, sir?"

"I am pleased to see you. I feel that I know you because word of your work with the trainees at Greystone University Hospital filtered down to the students in the law school. How can I help you?"

"Let me try to describe my problem. Since I insist that trainees in medicine organize the data they collect from patients, I feel I should organize the information I want to transmit to you in a coherent manner."

"Good, go ahead."

"First of all, my major problem is that I hold information that should be in the hands of the law. I can organize the information as follows:

"First, Dr. Baldwin and Dr. Colfax trained with me several decades ago. Since then they have practiced in the same building in Savannah. They were not financially connected, but they shared equally in paying for the overhead.

"Second, Dr. Baldwin was, and is, a quiet, hardworking, available, caring physician who orders only what is needed to diagnose and treat patients. He has no time to do anything else. He serves his patients well.

"Third, Dr. Colfax was, and is, a brilliant, aggressive, popular physician who orders an enormous amount of high-tech procedures because he receives a financial kickback from those who do the procedures. Some of his time is spent supervising a research project using a new medication for the treatment of hypertension. The drug was developed by MediSurge. Dr. Colfax makes a pile of money with his so-called research. MediSurge offered me $200,000 to join the project. I refused.

"Fourth, both doctors came to see me. Neither knew that the other had visited me. Each complained about the other, and Baldwin suspected that Colfax was not doing honest research. He supplied me with forms that had been filled out by Colfax. One of Baldwin's patients was listed on one of the forms, but Baldwin had not referred her to Colfax. The other forms listed patients who do not exist. I can prove that.

"Fifth, I feel trapped. Although I continue to be busy at eighty-five, I concluded that I should at least look into the matter because I felt obligated to protect the profession.

"Sixth, I visited their office in Savannah at Dr. Colfax's request. There was no doubt about it. Dr. Colfax's research was fraudulent. Ms. Hightower, who worked for Colfax, called me the next day and said she wanted to talk. She came to Atlanta and had lunch with me at the Cherokee Club. She confessed my worst fears. The research project was a sham. Her work was accurate, but Colfax changed her recordings to favor the drug they were investigating. I advised her to see the district attorney in the area. She was found dead in the ocean the next day."

James Smith replied, "Well done, Dr. Conley. I will call a lawyer friend of mine in Savannah and discuss—discreetly, of course—the problem, which ranges from fraudulent research to the possible murder of Ms. Hightower. I also will check up on MediSurge. I seem to remember that name. Were they not in trouble several years ago?"

"They were, but it is now under new management.

Smith stood up and said, "I will call you tomorrow with a plan."

"Thank you. In the meantime, I will be on alert because if Ms. Hightower was murdered, I am next in line."

Mr. Smith simply raised his eyebrows.

Vance left Smith's office for Brookland, arriving at 4:30 PM. Vance was convinced that his walking was deteriorating even more. He reflected on the deterioration of his walking. Initially, no one helped him open doors. As he became weaker and used a cane, young and middle-aged men looked at him and his cane and opened doors for him. Next, as he grew weaker, middle-aged women opened doors for him. Later, small girls opened the doors for him. Finally, elderly women looked him over and then opened the door for him. He always thanked whoever opened the door for him. He also noted that he could not open a screw-top bottle cap. He had to use pliers to open a bottle of water. All his muscles were weak, not just those in his legs.

Dinner was with Johnny, David, and Joseph. Delicious tilapia and sugar-free apple pie. There were two red roses standing on the table. Vance did not know the two ladies who had departed because they lived in their apartments and never went to the dining room. No one had signed up to attend memorial services for them.

Vance tipped his imagined cap to Jennifer and said, "Thanks for your help. I feel better now that I have the help of a very competent lawyer. I love you."

CHAPTER 16

Late October 2005
Midtown Atlanta

James Smith walked the floor thinking. What could he do as a lawyer to help his client, Dr. Vance Connelly? He was as devoted to the law as Vance was devoted to medicine. As he pointed out to Connelly, he would call his old classmate, Mary Collins, in Savannah. She would help them. She had made quite a name for herself.

The next day, Thursday, at 10:00 AM, Smith placed his call to Collins.

"Mary, dear, how are you?"

"I am just fine but too busy. How are you?"

"Doing well but too busy. I need your help."

"You have it."

Smith related the story to her. She never interrupted. When Smith was through, she asked, "Have you seen the morning paper? It may not be in your paper. Have you looked at television? It is all over our television."

"What, pray tell, is in the paper and on television?"

"Six patients have been admitted to one of the hospitals in Savannah with severe liver disease. Two of them are not expected to live."

"So?"

"They all had been taking a drug that Dr. Colfax was giving them in a research project sponsored and lavishly financed by a pharmaceutical and instrument company called MediSurge. The family members of the sick patients have already talked their heads off to our law firm. They want an investigation and a class action lawsuit against Dr. Colfax and MediSurge."

"My god. I suppose they will determine if Dr. Colfax or MediSurge knew if the drug damaged the liver. If they knew it might damage the liver but did not stop the study, they might all be in big trouble."

"If either knew the drug was causing liver damage but despite that continued the drug, you will see the biggest financial settlement in the history of medicine. You might even see the criminal charge—murder. If proven, then several people will be in the slammer forever."

"Can I tell my client that this tragedy has trumped his worry? He simply wanted a legal investigation to take place. This new event means that the investigation is already under way."

"Correct. You must tell him, however, that he may be asked to testify in court or elsewhere as the lawsuit gets under way."

"I am sure he will be glad to do that, and I will advise him to do so."

"It's been good talking with you. I miss Greystone. I remember Dr. Connelly too. I hope these events, tragic as they are, will offer him some relief."

"One other thing."

"What's that?"

"Remember, Ms. Hightower may have been murdered."

"I know. Be assured the sheriff's office will be notified, and the police will investigate that possibility."

"Thanks, Mary, thanks a load. See you."

"Good-bye, James. Hope to see you soon."

Vance had dinner with Johnny, Margo, Jan, Ralph, Grace, and Melvin.

No red rose tonight. The phone was ringing when Vance opened the door of his apartment. Vance struggled and hobbled to reach the phone before the person hung up. He just made it.

"Hello, Vance Connelly speaking."

"Hello, Dr. Connelly, this is James Smith." Smith related the story to Vance.

Vance frowned and said, "I am sorry to learn of the tragic deaths or serious damage that has occurred to those innocent patients. I had hoped that would be avoided. Now everyone can see what can happen when greed enters the picture. I will be glad to testify if I am needed."

"Fine, I knew you would say that."

"About Ms. Hightower?"

"The police are checking."

"Thank you."

"It was my pleasure to serve you."

Vance had more and more trouble taking the first step after sitting or standing. He had more trouble lifting a cup of coffee. He muttered, "Jennifer, you got me through another problem. I love you so. I continue to need your help."

CHAPTER 17

Early November
Brookland and Greystone

Three interns presented five patients at morning report. Vance said, as he studied the Problem Lists they had written on the board, "Excellent, to the point, clearly stated. These admissions are representative of a huge segment of America's sick. Note that the ages of the five patients are between seventy-eight and ninety-six years. Each patient has either heart disease, stroke, cancer, brain disease, or arthritis. Each, of course, has other diseases as well. The point is you must learn how to doctor these patients. They may not look at the world as you do. Are you able to detect and understand the psychological makeup of elderly patients? Do you know how to identify the early signs of dementia? Do you know the difference in the physiological behavior of an old heart compared to the physiological behavior of a young heart? Why is a heart attack worse in an old heart than the same-size heart attack in a young heart? I could go on and on. You must find out—know how your elderly patients and their families look at the world so you can discuss their medical care with them intelligently. Remember, there will come a time in every patient's life when they are slipping away and little can be done for them. That type of problem needs the best of doctors. Hope must be sustained, but comfort is virtually always needed. The goal for the doctor is to bring comfort to the patient and the patient's family, not to perform procedures that have no purpose or to give drugs for a possible miracle. Be there when the end comes when it is possible to do so. No other person can take your place. Please now, I hope I have raised many questions in your mind. Think about it. Think about it a lot."

Vance looked carefully at the young doctors—some of them heard him, and some of them did not.

As they left, Vance said, "Sorry for the sermon, but the care of the elderly is an important and very expensive part of medical care. By now you should have perceived that the care of the elderly has little to do with science and a lot to do with human relations."

Vance had a heavy load of regular mail, e-mails, and faxes. He left the office at 3:00 PM.

He checked his mailbox at Brookland. There was one letter and thirteen pieces of junk mail. All the residents at Brookland received an inordinate amount of junk mail. They threw it in a large trash can. They cuddled their real mail like it was a newborn baby and either read it like it was an emergency or took it to their apartment for uninterrupted time to read and savor its contents.

Vance had dinner with Johnny, Albin Darge, and his wife. Albin had been a very successful developer and had built many of the largest buildings in the city. He was a great and humorous conversationalist.

Vance entered his apartment just as the telephone was ringing.

"Hello, Dr. Vance Connelly speaking."

"Dr. Connelly, this is the wife of Dr. Baldwin in Savannah. I must tell you the bad news.

"Yes, Doris, go on."

Her voice cracking, she responded, "My husband committed suicide early this morning. He had been depressed. He had left the office before the scandal broke and simply could not cope with the deterioration of patient care that he felt was happening."

"Oh . . . oh, I am so terribly sorry. Can I help?"

"Well, yes."

"Anything."

"I would like for you to give the memorial address, which will be on Saturday two days from now at 2:00 PM at the Wesley Memorial Church on Victoria Drive."

"I will be honored to do so. Let me see now, I will spend the night at my place on St. Simons Island on Friday and arrive at your home at 10:00 AM Saturday. To get the feel of things, I want to talk with you, look at his home and books and any papers you feel free for me to see."

"That will be fine. You will bring comfort to me and the rest of the family. Good-bye, Dr. Connelly,"

"Good-bye. Again, I am so sorry. He was very good at all that he did." Vance had tears in his eyes and the feeling of grief. What a loss—it was all so sad—for the family and for the profession of medicine.

There was a fax from Johnny.

> Dolly—about 101 years old—is now on the second floor for extended care. We will miss her and her piano playing. See you in the lobby at 5:30.
>
> Johnny

After dinner, Vance returned to his apartment at 7:15 PM. He talked to Jennifer a long time. He reminded her of the three weeks they spent together in New Zealand. He mentioned the night a man played their favorite song on his mandolin. He then told her about Dolly. Vance, who was looking at Jennifer's picture, could swear that he saw her smile.

CHAPTER 18

November 2005
St. Simons Island, Savannah, and Brookland

Vance always felt close to Jennifer when he stayed in their condominium on St. Simons Island. Her loving and unique touch was everywhere. Her walking friends were sometimes there when Vance was there, but this Friday, he saw no one that he knew. Vance occasionally said in a semiaudible voice, "Jennifer, come back. I miss you so. We had such great times together here. Walking the beach, back when I could walk, eating at our favorite places, enjoying the sunset and sunrise. Can't we do it again, again, and again?"

Vance left Ship Watch on Saturday at 8:30 AM and arrived at Baldwin's home in Savannah at 10:00 AM.

Doris, Baldwin's beautiful wife, met Vance at the door of their modest home. "Dr. Connelly, thank you so much." She hugged him, and he held her for a moment.

Vance said, "Doris, I am so sorry. He was such a great person. That is what made him a great doctor."

"Let me introduce you to our family."

"Are they all here?"

"Yes. This is our son, John, and his wife, JoAnn, and their new baby. This is Mary, our daughter, and her husband, Jack."

"So pleased to meet you all. Dan was indeed blessed."

"I know you wanted to see Dan's study and look at his books and papers to get a feeling for his work and passion. Here is his small library and study room. He spent many hours in here. Would you like coffee?"

"That would be fine."

Doris brought Vance a cup of decaf coffee and left him with Dan's books, papers, and charts.

The library part of the room was filled with the classics of medicine. The books by Harvey, Heberdin, Sydenham, and Osler were there. Many of the pages of each of the books were tagged with yellow Post-it notes that marked Dan's favorite quotations. Baldwin kept his medical journals neatly arranged in the shelves above his computer. Vance noted that there were five patient charts stacked neatly at his worktable. He glanced through them all but avoided looking at the names of the patients. He was more than satisfied with what he saw. Baldwin knew his patients—all entries in the charts revealed his understanding of them as human beings as well as an understanding of their diseases.

Numerous friends were in and out of the house until it was time to leave for the church.

Doris said, "Dr. Connelly, please ride with me. John will drive."

"Fine, I would like to."

The church was filled with friends and former patients. At least four hundred or more people were already seated when the family and Vance arrived.

After a few minutes of music, the minister stood and then walked to the pulpit, where he introduced Vance to the congregation.

Vance, using his cane, walked slowly to the pulpit. He paused for a moment, looked from side to side, and began his memorial address.

"We are here to celebrate the life of Dan Baldwin. He came to work under my tutelage at Greystone University Hospital several decades ago. I had selected him, from among many applicants, because during my interview with him, I sensed that he was a solid thinker, had a keen sense of responsibility, and seemed to care about people. During his internship and residency, you could find him on the floor comforting his patients, recording every change he observed in the patient's record, and talking with the nurses about his patients' problems.

"I always ask the nurses how members of the house staff are doing. They often see a side of an intern or resident that no one else observes. Their report on Dan was always A+. He came quickly when they called him to see a patient. He learned from the nurses, and he taught the nurses. He recognized that many of the nurses had more experience than he did and, therefore, wanted to learn from them.

"The nurses said that they wanted Dr. Baldwin to be their doctor if they became sick. Patients would volunteer that Dr. Baldwin was their doctor. He had obviously learned that patients judge a doctor by assessing the characteristics they understand. Patients assume that their doctor knows what he or she is doing medically and scientifically. They judge the competence of a doctor by sensing if he or she is kind, honest, trustworthy, and available. Patients can sense if a doctor cares about them as a sick person. They loved Dan. Dan learned early that it takes two things to be a competent doctor. The doctor must know medicine but, in addition, must deliver what he or she knows in a caring manner.

"As I said, Dan learned that early in his career. Or perhaps, I should say, that he came to Greystone with that attitude. His mother and father had instilled those qualities in him.

"Later he brought those good qualities with him to Savannah, and many of you people here were the beneficiaries.

"I examined his personal library and home office today. He was a quiet scholar. He knew what had made the profession of medicine great. He knew why medicine is called the noblest of professions. He understood that he had to make a living, but he got his emotional kicks by delivering superb medical care. He loved his work and cared deeply for his patients, and his patients knew it. The medical records he produced on his patients are clear and concise. They reveal the sharpness of his mind and show that he cared enough for his patients to record his observations with equal care.

"May I digress and tell you about a tree on the Isle of Kos, one of the Greek islands. Hippocrates, the father of medicine, taught medicine on the isle of Kos some four hundred years before Christ. Legend holds that he taught under a certain tree. A few years ago, in 1980, I stood under one of the descendants of the tree of Hippocrates and taught medicine. My visit to the tree was part of a postgraduate course in medicine offered by Greystone University School of Medicine. As I viewed the tree in 1980, I thought it was a metaphor for the profession of medicine. The roots,

I thought, represented the basic beliefs that separate a profession of *service* from a mere job—or trade—or an occupation that involves the production of a product. The good doctor has no products to sell. He or she provides a needed service. I surmised that the leaves of the tree represented the doctors that deliver the service. When the roots are healthy, the leaves are bright and green. But the roots have become diseased. The profession has become a system that is composed of doctors, lawyers, industries such as pharmaceutical houses and instrument makers, government workers, and politicians. The doctors' work and environment are no longer controlled by doctors. Recent research and advancements have improved what medicine can do for patients, but the cost of medical care has increased beyond belief. There are many misguided souls who want medicine to be a business. So greed, frivolous lawsuits, fraud, and a businesslike approach have changed the profession. Accordingly, the leaves of the tree have gradually fallen to the ground.

"I saw Dan as the last leaf on the tree. More than any doctor I know, he struggled to deliver excellent medical care to his patients. He felt he could not decrease the time he needed to talk to patients. He would not order an expensive test that was not needed because he feared a lawyer might sue him. He did not prescribe expensive drugs when an old cheaper drug would do as well. He was unhappy when a patient left him, against his or her will, to go elsewhere for medical care because the patient's company that financed the medical care had cut a deal with another HMO that would save money but did not have Baldwin on their list of doctors. False advertising by drug houses troubled Dan enormously. Campaign financing by pharmaceutical houses for politicians who would vote in favor of a bill that favored a pharmaceutical house caused him grief.

"Recent events here troubled him emotionally. He was stronger than any doctor I know. I view him as being symbolic *of the last leaf on the tree of Hippocrates. Now the last leaf has fallen.*

"When he visited me in Atlanta, he talked of his love for his wife, Doris, his son and his family, his daughter and her husband. He also talked about you, his friends and patients. So to you I say, from my vantage point, Dan was one of the greatest doctors I have ever known, and that is because he was one of the greatest individuals that ever lived."

When Vance finished, there was not a dry eye in the sanctuary. Doris hugged Vance, as did the son and daughter.

Vance returned to his place in St. Simons and drove to Atlanta the next day.

He had dinner at Brookland with Johnny and Margo. He related the sad story to them. They too shed a few tears.

Vance looked at all the pictures of Jennifer. He said, "You were with me today. I could not have given the memorial address without your help. Your many years of guidance and influence were with me. Thank you. I love you."

CHAPTER 19

February 2006
Brookland, Greystone, and St. Simons Island

Vance noticed that his muscle weakness was increasing. He had more and more trouble opening doors. He had thought that some of the doors were locked because he could not open them. He almost fell on several occasions. One day he noticed that he could not open his right eyelid. He could, with a mighty effort, barely lift a cup of coffee. Getting up out of a chair was almost impossible. He noticed shortness of breath from moderate effort that he believed was due to weakness and fatigue of the thoracic and diaphragmatic muscles.

He made an appointment to see Dr. Quentin Jenkins. Vance had recruited Jenkins for the Department of Medicine many years earlier. Neurology was, at that time, in the Department of Medicine. Jenkins was now considered to be one of the nation's experts in neuromuscular disease. He was now a popular member of Greystone's nationally recognized Department of Neurology.

Jenkins arranged to see Vance promptly. Vance left his car with the valet at the hospital and tried to walk in the tunnel from the parking area to the building where Jenkins's office was located. He discovered he could not do it. He was forced to have his buddy, who supervised the valet parking, push him in a wheelchair to Jenkins's office.

"Vance, I am honored to see you. I have observed your problem from afar. What do you think is ailing you?"

"Quentin, I appreciate you seeing me so quickly. I am weak—my muscle strength is fading away despite exercise. My arms, fingers, legs are so weak I cannot function. I believe I either have neoplastic myopathy or myasthenia gravis."

"Have you lost weight? How is your appetite?"

"I have lost seven to eight pounds and have no appetite, which is unusual for me. Remember, I had cancer of the colon thirty years ago. I missed my last three-year colonoscopy because of my wife's illness, so I am worried about a new cancer of the colon that could cause neoplastic myopathy, but I actually suspect myasthenia rather than neoplastic myopathy. You know I had bilateral knee replacement about twelve years ago, but I don't believe my trouble is related to that because all of my muscles are weak. I can't use my fingers—I can't lift four pounds without a struggle. It is not just my legs."

Dr. Jenkins's neurological examination was negative except he identified that all Vance's muscles were weak.

"Have you had any eye signs?"

"My right eyelid would not open properly on one occasion this last week. That was strange—I could not understand why only one eyelid was affected rather than both if I had myasthenia gravis."

"Well, that can happen with myasthenia gravis. Even though a minority of patients have leg muscle weakness as the beginning symptom, we must rule out myasthenia gravis. I will schedule some lab work for you. We do have a blood test for the antibody that has inactivated the acetylcholine receptor site at the neuromuscular junction. Let's see if the antibody test is elevated. Although it is negative in a rather large number of cases, it is useful when it is positive."

"Good. Should we get a chest X-ray film since a thymoma is occasionally found in patients with myasthenia gravis?"

"We will get a CAT scan of your chest. Let me see you again in a week. Your lab work will be back then."

The lab work revealed very low serum albumin, severe anemia, an elevated blood calcium, and a negative test for the antibody against the receptor site at the neuromuscular junction. The CAT scan of the chest had not been done, but Jenkins scheduled Vance for an electromyogram.

The technician who performed the electromyogram was excellent. He pointed out that the test would take an hour or more and that it was painful but tolerable. The response to a series of increasingly strong electric shocks was recorded from most of the muscles in Vance's body. The response of the frontal muscle—the muscle above the eyelids located in the forehead— gave the signal that was usually found in patients with myasthenia gravis.

Dr. Jenkins was out of town for a few days, but when he returned, he called Vance to come to his office.

"Hello, Vance."

"Hello yourself. I know now why you went out of town. That test was painful."

He laughed and said, "Do you mind if I have a junior student join us?"

"Please do."

Jenkins revisited the entire case with the student who was listening and watching with considerable interest. Vance was impressed—Jenkins was a great teacher.

Jenkins said to Vance, "Now we will need to see if we get a therapeutic response. I will have you start on two types of medicine, and I will need your opinion about your response to them. You will have your CAT scan of the chest later today, I am told."

"OK, Quentin."

The CAT scan of the chest was initially read as normal, so Quinten conveyed the message to Vance. Vance was scheduled to go to Dallas. He made his plans to do so and confirmed the trip with the people he was to meet there for an editorial board meeting. Just after his plans were made, he received another call from Quentin, stating that the radiologist had called him and stated that on review of the CAT scan, he had identified a small tumor mass in the upper midsternum that was not located in the thymus. It was not a thymoma. Vance cancelled his trip. He had his secretary call his friends to state he could not be with them in Dallas.

By now, his friend, colleague, and former trainee, Dr. Gerald Worthy, was reviewing the record and talking with Jenkins. He was Vance's regular doctor and had been Jennifer's doctor through her three-month ordeal. Vance observed the superb care Gerald Worthy rendered his patients when he was a house officer and cardiology fellow. There was no better doctor. He suggested a consultation with Dr. Tom Allan, a thoracic surgeon. Worthy ordered a blood test for parathyroid hormone because Vance's blood calcium was elevated, and Allan ordered a special nuclear scan to study the parathyroids. Both tests were positive.

Vance, in his persistent teaching role, pointed out to his doctors how rare it was to have two rare diseases simultaneously. That would require much thought and an extensive search of the literature. Were they separate diseases, or was the myasthenia precipitated by the parathyroid tumor? Would removal of the tumor eliminate the weakness? There were only a few cases of that combination of diseases in the literature, and final answers had not been forthcoming.

Dr. Habor, an excellent and very experienced surgeon, removed the tumor from the chest by making a small incision above the right clavicle. He was truly an expert and had written a great deal about parathyroid adenomas.

Recovery from surgery was complicated by electrolyte problems, enormous edema from low blood albumin, muscle pain, and sleeplessness. Vance smiled because one of the interns he was teaching a week ago was assigned to examine him and implement his treatment. She proved her competence over the next few days.

Vance gradually improved and returned to Brookland where he was to have physical therapy three times a week for a month. He had meals brought to his apartment and worked hard in his exercise program.

Vance's old friend and partner, Dr. Robert Logan, who also lived at Brookland visited him often. He had taught Vance a great deal during the thirty years they worked together. He, being an excellent cook, prepared breakfast for Vance on several occasions. A technician came to Vance's apartment to draw blood for lab work. All abnormalities in the routine blood work gradually returned to normal. Vance returned to Greystone several times during the month of January but decided to return full-time on February 1, 2006. Vance needed a change in scenery, he thought. His middle son drove him to his place on St. Simons Island on January 14, where he planned to remain for two weeks. His son then flew back to Atlanta. Vance hoped to write and write and write because that habit had been interrupted by his illness and surgery.

He was overwhelmed with memories as he entered Ship Watch, where his condominium was located. Jennifer was everywhere. The feeling was overwhelming as Vance sat on the blue leather sofa the two of them had found and bought. He moved the furniture back to the places she wanted it to be. He said to himself, "Jennifer, I wish you were here."

He observed himself. He felt wonderful. The best he had felt in years. He could walk better than when he entered the hospital. He had no shortness of breath.

But he noticed that the strength in his legs and arms had plateaued following initial improvement. That is, his muscle strength was much better but had stabilized at a level that was far from normal. On two occasions, he noticed that he could not open the lid of his right eye. He was sure of it. Jenkins had advised him to take pyridostigmine bromide promptly if he developed what doctors call ptosis of the eyelids. Vance hurried as fast as he could to the row of medicine lined up on top of the bedroom chest of drawers. The right eyelid opened before he could take the medicine. The same event happened the next day. *Now what does that mean?* he thought. *It obviously forces one to favor myasthenia gravis, but it is still strange and atypical.* Vance planned to talk with several people when he returned to work on February 1. He wanted to talk with Jenkins, the neurologist; the surgeon, Gerald Worthy; and the chief resident in medicine at Greystone.

Vance thought the chief resident was the best problem solver he had seen. He also recognized that he was a superb teacher and clinical researcher. He had noticed how the young interns and residents flocked to him because he was a brilliant leader. Vance saw in him a future chairman of a Department of Medicine. Vance wanted to challenge him with the following questions:

- What thoughts do you have when one patient is believed to have two rare diseases?
- Since the medical literature does not answer these questions, what would you do to solve the problem and answer the questions?

Vance had dinner at Brookland with Johnny, Don, Jim, and David. There were strange names on the menu. Those who created the menu also created interesting and strange names for their dishes. This often caused a bit of interesting conversation.

Vance returned to his apartment at 7:05 PM. He stood up when he looked at each picture of Jennifer. He said out loud, "Jennifer, I am still sick. I may join you soon." He smiled as she seemed to smile back at him.

CHAPTER 20

Early March 2006
Greystone and Brookland

Morning report was brief because a visiting professor was scheduled to give a lecture in the large new Vance Connelly Cardiology Teaching Conference Room.

The nationally known visiting professor arrived with the pharmaceutical representative and three other drug house workers. Vance immediately calculated the expense of the lecture. The speaker probably received $1,000, plus travel expenses. The four drug house representatives were out-of-towners. Therefore, it probably cost each of them $2,000 or more to be present. The total expenses and honorarium probably cost between ten and fifteen thousand dollars.

The lecture itself was attended by about eighteen people. The subject was an old one that had been presented recently four or five times by other visiting professors.

The canned talk was a teaching failure, as are most lectures. Lectures, at their best, merely give an audience information. Lecturing is not the best way to teach clinical medicine. In fact, most lecturers do not know what they accomplish. Accordingly, they cannot be classified as true teachers.

When the lecture was over, one of the pharmaceutical representatives asked Vance, "How did you like the lecture?"

Vance, not wishing to offend the nationally recognized speaker and wanting to be noncommittal said, "He gave it a good try, didn't he?"

"Yes, yes. He was great. We use him a lot. Would you be willing to give us a statement about the drug he discussed? We are really proud of the drug."

"Well, not now, but see me in five years. By then, we will know if the drug is as useful as it seems to be now. Also, serious and unwanted side effects may be noted by then. I suspect the drug will not be used five years from now."

The speaker left with the pharmaceutical representatives. There was no contact with students, house officers, or faculty. Vance thought that the absence of contact might well have been a blessing. Vance concluded that the pharmaceutical houses were trying to take over medical education. Vance thought that every trainee must learn enough to question those who try to sell their wares. The modern pharmaceutical house reminded Vance of the enterprising men on the frontier of this country who sold snake oil as a definite cure for anything that ails one.

There was a letter waiting for Vance when he returned to Brookland. The letter was postmarked as being from California. Vance opened the two-page handwritten letter and noted that is was from Dr. Colfax. He thought to himself, *My god, my god, what is this?*

Vance read each sentence very slowly.

Dear Dr. Connelly,

You will note that this letter was mailed in California, but I am not in California. I had a trusted friend mail the letter from California because I am in a distant country that will not be named.

I am writing you with the hope I can, somehow, win my way back to a feeling of worthiness.

I am profoundly sorry for what happened. I deviated from your teaching and beliefs. At first, I bent my views only a little, but then because everyone else was making a lot of money by bending a little, I bent a little more, and soon, medicine was a business where success was judged by the amount of the bottom line. I gradually lost the joy I had felt during earlier days when I got my emotional kicks from delivering excellent medical care. My joy was fed by the bottom line, which never seemed to be enough.

I know now that I was wrong. I feel indirectly responsible for Dan Baldwin's death, but I did not kill Ms. Hightower. My bet would be that she was killed by a hit man hired by the very clever—and very dangerous—CEO of MediSurge.

Now that I am here in a poor country, I intend to set up a free clinic and treat the patients as you taught us to do. I will use the rather large amount of money paid to me by MediSurge to support me and my clinic. At least, the tainted money will be used to help those who can't help themselves.

I know the FBI will find me someday, and I will look for them every day of my life. I will return to the USA and do my time. But strangely, I am at peace with myself because I now recognize how wrong I was and plan to use my remaining time to help the people among whom I am living.

Forgive me please.

Gerald

Vance was stunned. He must now choose between keeping the letter secret or to turn it over to the police who were investigating the death of Ms. Hightower. He concluded he would have to turn it over to the police and, for the first time, felt sorry for Dr. Gerald Colfax.

Vance turned his thoughts toward his day—Saturday. He planned to make the trip to Middleton, his hometown, to visit with sick relatives, as well as classmates including one special friend whose husband had been his best friend.

Vance studied the photographs of Jennifer that were on the wall of his bedroom. So beautiful—radiating joy and kindness and love. He leaned against the chest of drawers and said, "Jennifer, I love you."

CHAPTER 21

April 26, 2006
Greystone and Arlington

Vance met with the interns and residents at Greystone University Hospital. Jennifer was on his mind because she had died on April 26 two years ago. He prayed for help to get through the day. Her qualities were on his mind as he looked at the somewhat anxious but eager faces of the young doctors.

Vance reviewed their rendition of their patient's diagnosis by studying the Problem Lists they had prepared on each of their patients. He was more than pleased with their work. They could not do that a few weeks earlier. They had evolved into much more thoughtful doctors. Vance congratulated them and decided to ask them a nonmedical question. The question needed answering and involved their future as well as the future of medicine as a profession.

Vance said to them, "You are smart. You can see what is happening. Many of the things that made the profession great—perhaps the greatest of professions—

174

have disappeared. How do you feel about it since the ball is now in your court? My generation owes your generation an apology. We could not stop the takeover. That is, other powerful forces have turned our profession into a business that is no longer controlled by doctors. Greed is prevalent, and medical care is not available to everyone. How do you feel about your future as a doctor?"

The members of the group looked at each other. One of them said, "Dr. Connelly, we do talk about this problem. We are for universal health care. We believe that every person—the poor and the rich—must have access to excellent medical care. We believe too that there should be a single-payer system. A doctor on the firing line of treating sick patients should not have to fill his office with expensive administrative staff who fight with several different payers. The single-payer system could be administered by the private sector although the track record of the private sector so far is very poor. So far, it is almost entirely profit oriented, and we don't believe that an unreasonable profit should be made off of sick people. The CEOs of the HMOs make double-digit millions of dollars each year. They get their massive raises by cutting services to patients who need medical care. So far, Medicare that is administered by the government has been the most successful. The patients can choose their doctor, which is a distinct advantage over the HMO. But of course, Medicare is only available for the elderly, and it must be updated because the amount paid to doctors by Medicare will not permit a doctor to keep his or her office open. Therefore, even Medicare needs updating. Still, it is a good model of a successful single-payer system of health care financing."

Vance was pleased at the knowledge the house officers revealed. Vance said, "Good thinking. But does that solve all of our problems?"

Another house officer spoke, "No, of course not. Most of us entered medicine because we wanted to help people. It is the only profession that combines science and humanism. So many of us were fascinated by science and also wanted to help people. We, in this room, have talked about this. We all still believe that the profession of medicine is about helping sick people. It is also about helping well people stay well. We are not in this to make a fortune. We could go into other fields if we wanted to do that. We want a reasonable life style and sufficient income to pay our debts that have accumulated over the last ten to twelve years of schooling and training, to be able to marry, to have decent homes, to have children, to have enough money to send the children to college, and to be able to retire after forty to fifty years of service. We want to spend more time with our patients to listen to their problems and to know how they react to their diseases. We are thrilled when we make a correct diagnosis and save a patient's life or simply improve their health. We get our kicks from the service we give, not from the financial aspect of activity."

Vance was even more pleased. He said, "You are the greatest." He choked a bit when he said, "You give me hope. I do hope also that your beliefs are felt by all of the house officers in this country! If you, the future decision makers in this country, believe that—and fight for your beliefs—then the proper future of the profession of medicine is assured. If you do not, the future of our profession is dismal."

Another house officer spoke up, "Dr. Connelly, we must have research and teaching. I would add, because I was a PhD-MD student, I hope to do research in oncology. The best research grants come from the National Institutes of Health. I favor that source for research funding rather than pharmaceutical houses. There is no bias or profit motive in the NIH grant system. The results are far more believable than the results of pharmaceutical sponsored research. Also, there needs to be a stable source of funds to pay for well-trained medical teachers. Currently, the teachers are pulled in too many directions. Many of them give lectures only—the same lectures they have always given. You have taught us—and I agree with you—listening to lectures is not the best way to learn medicine. We must, I believe, support superb medical teachers who can spend time with trainees."

Vance was even more surprised. "I had no idea that the house officers thought about such matters." He was profoundly relieved. He said, "I wish I could join your group. But the clock is ticking loudly for me. The future is now in your hands and in others like you. I congratulate you—you are wise."

Vance thought of the fifty-six years he had spent with house staff, students, and fellows. With a bit of moisture in his eyes, he said, "I love you all. I really do."

Vance met his middle son at Brookland. His son picked him up, and they traveled by car to Arlington. Arlington was a large cemetery. It was located in the outskirts of Atlanta. It was beautiful, serene, and meaningful to the families who used it. The date was April 26. The day Jennifer died two years earlier. Vance wanted to visit Jennifer's grave. It was drizzling, and the sky was dark but that did not stop them. His son helped him walk from the parked car to the grave. Vance and his son remained silent. Vance looked at the grave and thought, *Jennifer, I will never forget you. You are still with me. You influenced me. You are still influencing me, to be better than I would have been. My perception of the world would have been different had it not been for you. I know you will be interested in knowing that the current house staff perceive the current problems and are dedicated to improvement of the profession that you encouraged me to fight for. They are wonderful, young people. So, there is hope, and as you taught me, hope is as important as breathing. I love you.*

EPILOGUE

Vance was pleased that his muscle strength was better than it was prior to his hospitalization, but it was far from normal. A few weeks after surgical removal of the parathyroid adenoma, the parathyroid hormone blood level was still elevated. The doctors suspected vitamin D deficiency, which proved to be correct because the blood level for that vitamin was abnormally low. Vitamin D inadequacy can cause muscle weakness. Could that be the problem? This prompted a two-month period when Vance took large amounts of vitamin D and calcium. After two months, the vitamin D blood level had improved but was still low, and unfortunately, the parathyroid hormone blood level was still elevated and muscle strength remained poor. The plan was to continue treatment with vitamin D and to check the parathyroid blood level in two additional months. If, at that time, the parathyroid blood level was still elevated, tests for residual tumor and possible additional surgery might be needed. In the meantime, Vance tried several different dosage schedules for pyridostigmine bromide and could not tolerate it because of gastrointestinal complications. This occurred despite the use of hyoscyamine that tends to block the side effects. So the usual drug treatment for myasthenia gravis could not be tolerated. Vance noted two more symptoms that supported the diagnosis of myasthenia gravis— after a short nap in the late afternoon both eyelids remained closed after he woke up, and his neck muscles seemed to be weaker. This alarming event happened on several occasions. This supported the diagnosis of myasthenia gravis, but a definite diagnosis could not be made because Vance could not take the medication that usually improved the symptoms of that disease.

Accordingly, the final diagnosis was generalized idiopathic myopathy. Meaning, of course, that so far, a precise diagnosis cannot be made.

Vance suffered as he witnessed the humanitarian aspect of the medical profession fading away. He suffered even more when he realized that the same deterioration was occurring in all professions.

His memory of Jennifer grew stronger and stronger. He continued to say "Jennifer, come back" in an almost audible voice. He continued to call Saturday his day and traveled to his hometown to be with friends and family.

Hortense, the ruthless CEO of MediSurge, was indicted, tried, and found to be guilty of hiring a hit man to kill Ms. Hightower. She was sentenced to spend the remainder of her life in prison.

The hit man who killed Ms. Hightower was captured, indicted, tried, and found to be guilty and was sentenced to die in the electric chair.

Greystone University continued to grow. Endowment soared until the university itself ranked in the top twenty research universities in the United States.

Greystone University Hospital was consistently ranked among the best in the nation and the cardiology service ranked in the top ten. A new two-to-three-billion-dollar hospital and clinic campus was being planned.

Brookland continued to be the leader of retirement facilities and the large new addition was moving toward reality. Vance's friends at Brookland grew older, and some became red roses as the years passed. His friends there were priceless. Their love for each other sustained them as the years slipped rapidly by.

The profession of medicine changed greatly over the subsequent years. In fact, medicine was no longer considered to be a profession where service was rendered by well-trained physicians who cared deeply about the comfort and well-being of their patients.

The newest external force designed to destroy the profession was the pharmacy that advertised that patients no longer needed to see their doctor in order to obtain a prescription drug—they advised the patient to select the drug he or she wanted, and the doctor who worked for the pharmacy would sign the prescription.

The oxymoron was that the progress in medicine had made it possible to prevent, treat, and cure many diseases, but only a few people in the nation could afford the cost of modern medical care. The medical care of the elderly continued to deteriorate—nursing homes, retirement facilities, and old people in general were increasingly ignored. The profession of medicine had been smothered by greed and imperfect and fraudulent research along with deceptive advertising.

Lawyers were still suing doctors and hospitals. The pharmaceutical houses controlled members of the Senate and House of Representatives by controlling campaign financing. This in turn guaranteed that members of the congress would cast their votes in favor of the pharmaceutical house. The FDA was also in the pocket of the pharmaceutical house.

As years passed, medical education, hospitals, and medical schools changed because pharmaceutical houses and instrument makers controlled their finances.

Vance concluded that the death of Dr. Dan Baldwin was symbolic—*the last leaf had fallen from the tree of Hippocrates.*

Vance believed that a new tree of Hippocrates would spring from the earth. That was a tree filled with hope. Its roots and leaves would be healthy and strong. They would symbolize the best of mankind. They would represent kindness, honesty, integrity, and a desire to serve the needs of others as well as being intelligent and wise. How will this be done? Vance smiled as he thought of the brilliant and kind trainees he had known. He had

unshakable faith that the trainees he knew, taught, and loved would do the right thing. They would correct the mess that had been left them.

They would favor universal health care and would deliver it in a compassionate manner.

Printed in the United States
98135LV00002B/26/A